**Other APPLE® PAPERBACKS
you will want to read:**

SHORT SEASON

SCOTT ELLER

AN
APPLE®
PAPERBACK

SCHOLASTIC INC.
New York Toronto London Auckland Sydney

*For Gordy and Lee,
and for all the boys and girls
with whom I've played ball.*

ISBN 0-590-33573-1

12 11 10 9 8 7 6 5 4 3 2   5 6 7 8 9/8 0/9

Printed in the U. S. A.

Chapter 1
Dean

I saw the kid at the plate swing and the ball left the bat and hurtled upward. At first I couldn't tell which way it was heading, but when I heard the sound — a sharp sound — I knew for sure it was coming toward me in right field. I watched it arc up and level off. It seemed to be just floating or drifting across the blue sky. Then it started down. I moved to my left, stopped, and turned to my right. I moved back toward the fence. The ball began to get bigger, and I realized I had no idea where in right field it was going to come down.

I picked a spot and stood there and put my glove up over my head and waited.

They had a base runner on second and only one out, and if I dropped it we'd be in a tie ballgame. But I wasn't too worried. Dean hadn't let me drop a fly ball all season.

The ball was growing larger, spinning slowly, and I could see its red laces. It seemed to be coming right at me. Maybe I'd catch this one after all.

But then I heard footsteps pounding on the hard

clay, and a shadow flashed in front of me, and I heard the *smack* as the baseball hit Dean's glove and I saw him wheel, turn, and throw, and the ball rocketed away toward the infield almost in a straight line. U.L. was there at second to take the peg with his foot on the bag like a first baseman, and that was it. The runner had gone halfway to third and Dean had thrown him out cold. We were out of the inning.

We were playing the Bolton White Sox. They were good, but we had beaten them once before and we were pretty sure we could do it again. They were giving us a tough game. Their hitting had improved, and they'd managed to score four runs. We'd scored five. If we could win this game, we'd have a good shot at the championship. If not, they'd have a shot at it. We were tied with them for second place in the league, just one game out of first place.

I trotted off the field behind Dean. Dwight tried to give him a high five as he went by, but Dean looked the other way. Everybody crowded around the bench and Coach yelled: "All right, listen up! Numbers eight and nine, Dean Harris and Hobbs, batting first and second. Then the top of the order, you know who you are. Let's go, gentlemen. Let's score some runs. We need 'em. Don't let up now — you got two tough innings to go." He looked down the bench. "Dean — ?"

Dean was sitting at the far end. He was leaning forward with his head down. He looked up.

"Where's your bat?" Coach said. "Come on, look alive, you're leading off."

Dean stood up.

U.L. Reed, our shortstop, was rubbing his left palm. He said to Dean: "Man, what'd you load that arm with today? You tore my hand off!"

But Dean didn't acknowledge the compliment; he just grabbed a bat. I noticed it wasn't even his own bat. It was Herd's, and I didn't think Dean would do any better with that one. It wasn't right for him.

He was batting eighth because he wasn't a good hitter. I wondered whether he was depressed about that: lately he'd been in a worse slump than usual, with no hits in our last three games. But not hitting had never seemed to bother him before. He accepted it, same as I accepted the fact that I wasn't the best fielder on the team. Some things you just learn to live with, like rain and mosquitoes.

Dean's my older brother. He's thirteen, I'm twelve. We're only about eleven months apart, in age. It's weird, but I can usually tell how he's feeling just by looking at him. Sometimes I don't have to see him to know. I can just hear him — hear his tone of voice, say — and I know exactly how he feels, maybe even know what he's thinking.

That's because we're so close in age, even though he's older. When he says something he doesn't mean, I know it right away.

But looking at him now — seeing the way he sat on the bench, and the way he grabbed Herd's heavy bat — I couldn't tell what was bothering him. I knew something was, but I didn't know what.

John Hobbs picked up a bat, too, and walked over to the dusty on-deck circle. This was the Little League field, and it was August, and the sun had turned the clay rock hard and dried the grass up and really almost killed it. But the infield wasn't bad, no holes and not too rocky, and we didn't mind playing here.

Dean set himself at the plate and peered out at the White Sox pitcher. Their infield was talking it up; they sounded like a bunch of girls, their voices high and whiney: "Hey, come on, Ronnie, come on, kid, you can do it, be a pitcher in there big guy," all the stuff that doesn't do your pitcher any good, not really, and their Ronnie wound up and threw the ball past Dean for a called strike.

Dean stepped out of the box for a second and looked over at Coach at first base.

Coach clapped his hands, then cupped them at his mouth, which means, "hit away." "Come on, Dean," he hollered. "Just a single, kid, get something started."

4

Dean stepped back in, and their pitcher wound up and threw and Dean took ball one. That made me proud of him. One of the hardest things a hitter can do is take a close pitch for a ball after you've taken a strike. But he did it, and now he had him at one and one. The next pitch was low for two-and-one, and I really thought Dean would get on base this time. He'd either get a fat pitch to hit, or he'd walk. And he did: the next pitch was a nice slow fastball right down the pipe, but Dean was taking all the way. Strike two. On the next pitch he chased a slow curve that was inside as well as low, and he looked pretty bad. He struck out going after a bad pitch, and I felt sorry for him.

Dean walked over and slumped down on the end of the bench. I didn't think I ought to talk to him.

If there was anyone on the team who hit worse than Dean, it was John Hobbs. Coach gave him the bunt sign. Coach has two bunt signs, and this one was the bunt-toward-third sign. John Hobbs was quick, and their third baseman was playing pretty far back. Maybe he could get on base that way.

The next thing that happened was pretty amazing. I guess it's why I like this team so much. All the guys do stupid things now and then; that's only natural. You make a bad play, or do something dumb, and, well, we all do it. That's part of playing Little League. You make mistakes. But one reason I love to play is this: Every now and then one of the guys on the team does something amazing. They'll make a play you didn't think they could make and it just knocks you out.

Anyway, what John Hobbs did was swing at the first pitch as hard as he could. He sliced at the ball viciously with his bat, and as he followed through on his swing he almost fell down. He was faking, trying to make the White Sox think he was going for the long ball. I'd never heard Coach tell anyone to fake it, and when I saw him do it I somehow knew what he was up to and knew that he'd made it up himself.

Solly Ehrmann was sitting next to me on the bench. Solly said, "Hey! What's he doing? Didn't Coach give him the bunt sign?"

"Shut up, fool," said U.L. He was in the on-deck circle, kneeling down on one knee, a toothpick hanging out of his mouth. "They can hear you way over on their bench."

"He did it on purpose," I said quietly. "Just watch."

Sure enough, John Hobbs bunted the next pitch. He laid it down toward third and scrambled out of the batter's box. Both the third baseman and the catcher got a slow start; they were taken completely by surprise. The ball dribbled toward the foul line, and their catcher, who got there first, decided to let it roll foul. He bent over and watched it roll, and it stayed fair. Just then a couple of our

6

guys began to whoop and yell, and I looked over and Coach had sent John Hobbs on to second. The third baseman shouted something and the catcher picked up the ball and turned and threw to second, but his throw was high, and John Hobbs slid under the tag, safe and sound. He'd bunted for a double.

Now U.L. was up and I was on deck. All of us were getting pretty excited. We had a man on second with only one out, and the top of our batting order was coming up. I went down to get a bat and there was Dean, sitting by himself at the end of the bench, not really paying attention to anything.

"Wish me luck," I said. "Your brother's going to be a hero. I'll make you famous."

He looked up, and I got the weirdest feeling. He stared at me and his eyes looked sort of watery. I'd never seen that expression on his face before. I felt like I didn't know who he was. It was the first time I'd ever felt that way, and it scared me. He looked at me in a way I didn't recognize, and I didn't know who he was or what he was thinking.

Then he said, very softly and clearly, "Go away."

I picked up my bat and walked out to the on-deck circle.

For a few seconds I had a hard time concentrating on the game. I didn't know what to do, and I didn't know what to think. I watched U.L. foul off a couple pitches, and then suddenly I didn't care about the game, I just wanted to know what was wrong with Dean. I looked back toward the bench, trying to get another glimpse of him, but I couldn't see him. There was nobody there on that end of the bench. Dean had disappeared.

U.L. took a good cut at the next pitch and hammered the ball into right field. The right fielder was playing pretty shallow, though, so Randy Bell, who was coaching third, held up John Hobbs. U.L. didn't try for second.

So when I came up, there were men on first and third and only one out.

I felt angry at Dean by this time and I wanted to knock the stuffing out of the ball. The first pitch came hissing in real fast, but it was high and I didn't swing. The ump called it a strike, though, so I stepped out of the batter's box and gave him a dirty look. It was a bad call, but I didn't say anything. I got set again and tried to ignore the chatter of their infielders. I watched their big pitcher go into his stretch. Then he threw over to first base, and U.L. got back in time. I stepped out and remembered to look at Coach. I watched his signals, but he was only telling me to hit away. The next pitch was a fastball inside. I opened up my stance a little bit — stepped out toward third base — and socked that fastball down the line past the third baseman. I ran like a maniac toward first, and the coach waved me on and I churned toward second. I saw the left fielder pick up the ball and throw toward home; when the shortstop let the ball go past him, over his head toward home plate, I tried for more speed and headed around second for third. I saw U.L. slide in ahead of the ball; saw the catcher catch the ball, look back at U.L., and then look toward second; saw his face change when he saw me heading toward third; saw him stride forward and throw. That's when I hit the dirt: I slid, felt my foot hit the bag, then felt a glove hit me in the knee. The ump yelled, "Safe!" and I thought, that's the best call he's made all game.

Everybody was fired up now, but Kenny Eades swung at a bad pitch and hit a hard bouncer right at the third baseman, so I couldn't score. Then Herd came up and bashed a line drive between short and second, and I came in with the third run of the inning. I got congratulations from everybody on the bench, all of them slapping me and shouting, even Dean, who had somehow appeared as mysteriously as he had disappeared. "Nice going, Brad," he said. "Good baserunning." He seemed his old self again.

Soon we were jogging back to the outfield. "What happened?" I asked. "Where'd you go?"

He gave me another one of those weird looks.

"Dean?" I said.

He flipped me the practice ball.

"Come on," I said. "Where'd you take off to?" I tossed him the ball.

"Stuff it, Brad," he said. "I went for a drink of water. What's the matter with you?" He threw me a fly ball, and I ran after it and dropped it. "You ought to learn how to catch," he shouted at me, suddenly. I stared at him. Then I thought back. Had I done something? Said something? He'd never gotten down on me about my fielding before. Why now?

The rest of the game isn't worth telling about, except for a couple of things. Dean batted again in the bottom of the sixth. There were two outs and nobody on base, and we had a four-run lead, so nobody really cared if we scored any more runs. Dwight was pitching well and we only had one more inning to go. But when Dean stood up at the plate, you could tell he was tense. He was using his own bat this time. He's left-handed, and from our bench I couldn't see his face, but I could tell by the way he was standing in the batter's box that he really wanted to get a hit.

Of course, that's the last thing you want to do as a hitter, is get all tense up there. Sure, you've got to concentrate, and you've got to *want* to get a hit, but it doesn't help to get so tense about it. That just makes things worse.

This time Dean wasn't going to take any pitches. He swung at the first pitch and only got a piece of it. He swung at the second pitch, too, and hit it straight up. The catcher caught it.

So we went into the top of the seventh. Dean and I tossed the ball around the outfield, not talking, and they finally got a batter up, a pinch hitter, a big kid who probably couldn't field, like me. He hit a soft line drive that dropped just in front of Kenny for a hit. Then there was another hit and then a walk, and with the bases loaded, Dwight looked shaky. He walked the next batter, which forced in a run and put the go-ahead run at the plate. With the score eight to five, Dwight knew he had to throw strikes and hope they hit the ball to us and not between us.

Anyway, the next kid up hit a single right at me, and as I moved in to field it, I heard Dean say, "Give it to me," and this was nothing new, we'd done this plenty of times, so I caught the ball on the second or third hop and flipped it to Dean and he fired it home and, sure enough, Herd put the tag on the guy trying to score.

Two outs.

That surprised Bolton. They were up for a big rally, and Dean had just wiped it out.

Next up was the number-four hitter, one of their best. He was a lefty, so I played almost on the line, and Dean moved over toward me. He could cover most of right field as well as center, and that was our routine: When a lefty batted, he went after every ball that wasn't right down the line. Once or twice he'd actually caught pop flies in foul territory. He was that good a fielder, and I was that bad.

Anyway, this left-handed kid on their team was swinging for the fences. He hit a shot down the line toward me that landed just barely foul and skipped past me. That worried me. It was hot enough out there as it was, but now I really started to sweat. I was afraid he was going to hit one fair that I couldn't handle, and that would be the game. They'd win on my bad fielding. He stepped up to the plate again and, sure enough, he was going for the right field foul line. He smacked that thing just as hard as he could, but he got under the ball a little and it hung up in the air. It wasn't really a high fly ball, it was still a line drive, but it had a loop to it even though it'd been hit hard and was carrying a long way. Seeing it take off like that gave me a sinking feeling. The ball headed for the corner, but it was going to be fair, and it had a good chance of leaving the park altogether. I started backing up for it, but then I heard Dean: "I got it, I got it!"

I stopped where I was and stood still and watched. Dean was going full speed, racing back toward the fence and the foul line. His eyes were fixed on the ball and his legs were churning so fast they blurred. He seemed to know exactly where to run, and when he got back to the fence the ball was just arriving — a long, thin streak of white — and he reached across his chest with his right hand and stabbed his glove out and the ball slapped into it like there was no one spot on that field or in the whole town of Adrian or on the planet Earth where that ball belonged but in Dean's glove.

We all swarmed around him, and the game was over.

I ought to say one thing about Dean. He was good but he wasn't the star of the team or anything. We had plenty of good players: Kenny Eades; Davey Pearson; U.L., with his great arm; Dwight, with that curve of his; John Hobbs; Solly Ehrmann, at first, who'd worked the hidden ball trick a couple of times that season; and our catcher, Andy Lawler, whom we called "Herd."

Dean did play a great center field, though, and it so happened he played a great right field, too, both at the same time. He caught just about everything that came in our direction. I wasn't too good in the outfield, but I was a worse infielder. I could hit, though. I was batting over .500 on the day we played Bolton, and that hit in the fifth that scored two runs boosted my average to .526. Coach wanted me in the line-up for sure, no matter what kind of — as he used to say — "atrocities" I'd do with my glove. I looked *atrocities* up in the dictionary.

So Dean and I complemented each other just fine. He couldn't hit, and I couldn't field; he could field and I could hit. He didn't really have to hit the ball because he had such a great arm, and he could catch anything. It didn't much matter what he did at the plate. And it didn't matter what I did in right field, either, because Dean was always there to make the play. So I didn't worry much about my fielding. It was pretty bad, though.

After we beat the Bolton White Sox that day in August, and after we swarmed around Dean, whose catch had ended the game, Coach called us over to the bench. He said he wanted to talk to us.

We went over and sat down on the old bench. We were in a real good mood and Coach had a hard time shutting us up. But we finally quieted down and listened.

"You've got a shot at this thing," he said to us. "You're playing good ball and you're only a half game out of first place. You beat a good team today, one of the other contenders. You can go all the way."

"Yeah! Go all the way!" Herd shouted. The others laughed. Coach paused and gave us his bored look. We shut up.

"What I'm saying is this. You may not be the greatest thing in the history of Michigan, but you can win this thing if you want to. You've got the talent and I think you've got the desire. But you have to win all the rest of your games. You'll be playing some top teams during the next few days — not just the Cardinals, but the Giants, and then the Pirates. We're going down to the wire, but you can control it if you want to. You can win it all. But you've got to win every game.

"That may sound like a lot, but it's not. You won today because you played good ball. Everyone did his share. Dwight pitched a great game. When he got in trouble, I think of his last eight or nine pitches, only one was a ball. That's perfect, that's just what I want in the late innings. Brad? What can I say? You now have the highest batting average in the league."

I felt good. Herd was sitting next to me, and he nudged me.

Coach went on. "Solly, you're doing fine, playing a good, solid first base. Dean — keep up the fine work in the outfield. You saved us three or four runs today with your defense; that's just what we want from you. You're playing great baseball. Herd, that goes for you, too."

"Aw, I was terrible," Herd said.

"Don't let one lousy passed ball get to you. You know better than that. You're doing too many things well to let one mistake bother you. Who'd I forget? U.L.? When are you going to get the toothpick out of your mouth, U.L.?"

Everyone laughed. U.L. removed the toothpick that was sticking out of the side of his mouth and tossed it over his shoulder.

"Well, anyway," Coach said, "you and Hobbs

turned two double plays today. We'll need more of them down the stretch. Keep it up.

"Okay. That's about all I have to say. We've got Ubly tomorrow. The Cardinals. Game time two o'clock. Be here at one. Any questions?"

There was a pause. Dean was sitting at the end of the bench. He stood up.

"Coach," he said, "can I say something?"

"Sure, go ahead."

I looked at Dean. I don't know exactly what it was, but I knew something was coming. It was his expression, I guess. He looked like something terrible had just happened.

He stared down at the ground and pushed some loose dirt around with his spikes. "Well, I just want to say this. I don't know how to say it. It's nothing against you guys, and nothing against you either, Coach." He looked up. He looked like he hated us all, or hated being there. "But I can't play anymore. I'm quitting. This was the last game. I hope you guys win it." We were all staring at him, not believing what we were hearing.

Then his face closed off. Instead of looking embarrassed or sorry, he just looked blank. "That's it. I'm quitting. See you guys around."

And with that, my brother turned and walked off the diamond.

Chapter 2
Mom

When I got home that afternoon, our street looked different. So did the house. I guess it was because Dean wasn't with me.

I rode up the street toward the house. We lived on a quiet street almost out of town. Our house was older than I was. Mom and Dad had bought it before Lisa, my older sister, was born, and we weren't the first owners. So it must have been twenty years old or more. The other houses on the street looked pretty much the same. I know that bothers some kids, living in a house that looks like all the others on the block, but it never bothered me. I knew the insides were different, with our own stuff and everything. The people inside were different, too.

But that afternoon the street didn't look the same. I'm not sure what was different. The sun was setting and it hit the trees and turned them orange. But that wasn't it.

I was alone. Usually Dean and I rode home together, after a game or a practice, or after school. When I rode into the driveway that afternoon, the garage door was up and there was Dean's bike, a red one with no fenders, already put away. So he was home. I leaned mine against it, slid by Dad's old car — an old Model A Ford — and closed the garage door.

The trees around the house and garage looked more bare than usual. I don't know how to describe it. The house didn't look so much like home. The grass was short and almost brown; the big maple tree in front of the house looked smaller, not as leafy, not stretching over the house the way it usually did. The other houses on the street were farther apart. The shrubs and bushes around the house and garage were thin, and you could see right through them. Mom had planted flowers outside the front door, by the walk, and I really liked them; they added color. That evening they looked scrawny and ugly. So did the house. It looked small. There was paint chipping off the garage and, where Dad had patched holes in the window screens, some of the patches were coming off.

I walked around to the back and went inside. I took off my spikes in the back hallway. There was a closet for Dean and me and, when I put my glove and spikes and bat away, I noticed that Dean's stuff was already in the closet. He was probably up in our room. But I didn't want to speak to him. Not yet.

I went into the kitchen. Mom was there. She's kind of plump. She has dark hair and she's soft where you lean up against her, and she always smells good.

She was sitting at the kitchen table reading a book. There was food cooking on the stove.

"Hi, Mom." I leaned against her.

She put her arm around me. "Hello, Braddy."

"When did Dean get home?"

"Ten minutes ago." She looked up at me. "Where were you? How come you two didn't come in together?"

"I don't know."

"How was the game? I hear you won."

"Yeah. It was all right. Dean say anything?"

"Not much." She looked at her watch. "Go on, now. Your father's due home any minute. Hurry and wash up. I'll call you in a while."

She gave me a little shove out of the kitchen.

Upstairs, Lisa's door was shut as usual, and she was playing rock music, as usual.

Our door was closed, too. I opened it and went in.

Dean was lying on his bed, staring up at the ceiling. He had taken off his uniform and put on blue jeans and a T-shirt. The T-shirt said ADRIAN BASEBALL. It was too big for him, and it was brand new.

"Where'd you get that?" I said.

He shrugged.

I stood in the doorway for a moment, looking at him. He didn't say anything. I went back out the door and down the hallway to the bathroom. Dad's car pulled into the driveway while I was cleaning up.

When I got back to our room, Dean was still on the bed. He hadn't moved.

"Nice catch today," I said.

It was a dumb thing to say. It was something you'd say to a stranger. But that's how I felt — like I was talking to a stranger.

"Thanks," he said.

"How come you're quitting the team?"

"I don't want to talk about it."

"Why not?"

"Because."

"Come on!" I went over to the bed and stood over him. I felt like hitting him. "Why won't you tell me?"

"Leave me alone, will you?" He turned over.

I hated him. "Okay. I'll leave you alone." I slammed the door as I went out.

Dinner that night was chicken. I still had on my Adrian Orioles uniform, and Dad was still wearing his tie.

Lisa was talking about a problem she had with some girl, a friend of hers or something. This girl was friendly with a boy she wanted to meet, but she wouldn't introduce Lisa to the guy. I didn't hear much of the conversation. Finally Dad said, "Wasn't there supposed to be a game today? Dean? Brad?"

I looked at Dean. He kept eating. I said, "Tell Dad about the game, Dean."

"We won. Eight to six." He kept on eating.

"Good going," Dad said. "Get any hits?"

"No."

"Brad?"

"Yeah, I got a few. Tell him what happened after the game, Dean."

"Shut up!"

"Boys," said Mom. She looked at Dad, then at me. "Brad, that wasn't fair."

"You know about it?" I said.

"Yes, I do."

I couldn't believe it. She hadn't said anything when I came home. "Well, why don't *you* tell Dad then, since you know so much."

"Tell me what?" said Dad.

"I quit the team, Dad. Hear that, Lisa? I quit the team. Now does everybody know? You satisfied, Brad?"

"No! I want to know why!"

"Brad," said Mom, "that's enough. Try to talk civilly to your brother. Does he have to report to you in full about *everything*?"

"But, Mom," I said, "he quit in front of the whole team. No one knows why. And we've only got three more games left, and if we win them, we'll be in the playoffs."

"Definite end-of-the-world stuff," said Lisa.

"It *is*, Lisa." I was mad.

"So how come you quit the team?" Dad asked Dean. I cheered, but silently, to myself.

Mom gave Dad one of her looks.

Dean got up and walked out of the dining room.

Dad went off somewhere after dinner. So did Lisa. Someone came by in a car and picked her up. Dean made a phone call and I didn't know who it was to. I helped Mom with the dishes.

After we were finished she went into her bedroom and shut the door. Dean was downstairs watching television, so I went up to our room. Dean's uniform lay in the corner, neatly folded even though it was dirty. I looked at his desk. There were books, a pencil holder, a pad of paper, and a blotter all lined up. Dean was something that way. I used to move things — slide a pencil around, put his bat in another part of the room — and he'd always go, "You're not funny, you know that?" when he found out. Anyway, the pad had a phone number written on it, and the number was circled. Dean had doodled on the pad, drawn x's and o's all over it. I wondered whose phone number it was.

I went down the hall and knocked on Mom's door.

She was sitting at her desk. The windows were open to let in the evening air and the twilight.

"What are you doing?" I closed the door.

Mom leaned back and sighed. "I'm trying to figure out which bills to pay this month and which ones to put off till next." She smiled at me, but it wasn't a real smile.

"Do you want me to leave?"

"No, Braddy. Stay. Want to talk?" She closed her checkbook and put down her pen.

"I guess so." I went and sat on the bed. Mom turned around and looked at me.

Then I couldn't think of anything to say. That's what happens. You finally get somebody's attention, but all of a sudden you forget what you wanted to say to them.

"Is it about your brother?"

"Yeah."

"What about him?"

"I don't know. He's acting so weird."

She smiled. "Yes, I suppose he is."

"What's wrong with him, Mom?"

"I don't know. Ask him."

"I did already. He won't tell me."

"Oh. Well? . . ." She raised her eyebrows.

"Why'd he quit the team?"

"I really don't know, Brad. Only he can tell you that."

"But he won't."

"Well then, you'll have to be patient. Wait till he's ready to tell you."

"But he always tells me things. He never acted this way before. What do you think's the matter?"

"Well, Braddy, maybe he's growing up. He's older than you are, after all."

"Well, not by much."

"No, but one year can make a lot of difference."

"He's not a year older. Eleven months."

"Okay. Almost a year. And you're growing up, too, don't forget. Both of you are. Grown-ups don't always tell each other everything that's on their mind."

"Aw come on, Mom. We ain't grown up."

"Aren't. Perhaps not. But you're getting there."

"So what? What's that got to do with anything?"

"Well, perhaps Dean has other things on his mind besides baseball."

"Like what?"

"I don't know. You've just got to be patient. He'll talk to you about it soon, I'm sure he will."

"Yeah, but you don't understand, Mom. We need him on the team. We're going for the division title this week. We've got to win every game. We can get into the playoffs, except. . . ."

I looked down at my hand. The bedspread on the bed was white and it had little knots on it. My hand was tugging at the knots. I stopped and folded my hands in my lap.

"Except what, Brad?"

"I don't know. I just don't think we can do it without him." Now I felt like crying. "I don't know how I'm gonna play the outfield without Dean there. He's so good, and I — I stink!"

Mom got up and went into the bathroom. She came out with a box of tissues. I blew my nose.

"Thanks."

She kissed me and sat down again.

"So what will you do?" she asked me.

"I don't know. I don't wanna play without Dean."

"Oh, Brad."

"I don't!"

She just looked at me.

"Why should I? He always makes all the catches. Now Coach'll probably put Randy Bell in center field. He's a creep."

"Well, if he does, you'll have to get used to it, won't you?"

"No. I'll quit, too."

"Oh? Why?"

"Well, why'd Dean quit?"

"That's his business."

"I don't want to play without him."

"All right."

That surprised me. "Do you mean that?"

"Of course I do. If you don't want to play without Dean, you don't have to. But sooner or later you're going to have to learn to get along without your brother. One way or the other. He won't always be on the same team with you, Brad."

"Sure he will."

"I doubt it." She smiled again. "Anyway," she said, "wouldn't you rather play than quit? Even if Dean doesn't play, don't you have fun? And you're such a good hitter. The team would miss you terribly. What's your batting average these days?"

"Five-twenty-six."

"Why, Brad, that's wonderful!" she said. "You're hitting so well!"

"Mom. I don't want to stop hitting. I just don't want to play right field without Dean in center."

She chuckled. "I see."

I looked around the room. It seemed empty, somehow. "Where's Dad?" I asked.

"I don't know. Out somewhere." She looked at the bills on her desk.

"You don't know where he went, Mom?"

"Not exactly. He said he had work to do."

"He's gone a lot of the time."

"He's very busy these days, Brad." She didn't sound too pleased about it.

I got up off the bed and walked around the room. It was pretty big, larger than Dean's and mine. There were a couple of bureaus along one wall, and a bathroom of their own, and two big closets. Her desk was opposite the foot of the big double bed where they slept. I walked around the bed and opened the door to Dad's closet.

The inside was stuffed with shoes and pants and coats. Some of the shirts said FORD on them. Dad ran a Ford dealership. There were hats and sweat-shirts on the shelves, and a pile of dirty laundry on the floor.

I looked over at Mom. She was working at her desk again, so I went and opened the door of her closet. Hanging up were dresses and skirts and blouses, packed pretty tight. A lot of belts hung from a hook, all different colors. Mom's shoes were neatly lined up on the floor around the walls of the closet, in a horseshoe shape. She must have had fif-teen pairs of shoes.

I shut the closet door and went and stood next to her. She looked up.

"I guess I'll play tomorrow."

She nodded.

"What can I do now?"

She sighed. She laid down her pen and put an arm around me. "Take a shower. Why don't you think about going to bed?"

"Too early."

"What's Dean doing?"

"I don't know. Probably watching TV. I don't care. I'm never going to talk to him again."

"I doubt that."

"I'm not." I shrugged her arm off my shoulder and pulled away from her. "Look, can't you say something to him? He's got to play. These are im-portant games. Come on. He can't just quit!"

She looked me straight in the eye. "No, Brad. I

can't make him play. You're both old enough to make some of your own decisions."

"You won't talk to him?"

"No. I'm sorry."

"Thanks a lot." I walked out. But I closed the door softly. I felt pretty good about our talk, even if she wasn't going to talk to Dean for me.

Dean wasn't in our room. Dad wasn't home yet. I went downstairs to the living room, and I could hear the sound of the TV coming from down in the basement. I went out the front door and sat on the lawn, under the maple tree.

It was almost dark. The sky was a purple color with a few bright stars. It was cool now, and there was a breeze. I could hear a dog barking way off somewhere, but other than that, our neighborhood was quiet.

I could go talk to Dean, I thought. But it wouldn't do any good. He'd just get mad and tell me to leave him alone and let him watch TV, and then I'd want to hit him. Maybe Mom's right. Be patient. Maybe he'll come back on his own. Maybe he's just kidding, playing a joke on everyone. That'd be great. I'd kill him if he was just joking. Another game tomorrow. The Cardinals, from Ubly. They've got some lefties who can really hit. Big guys. A lot of balls in the outfield. Maybe he isn't really quitting. Maybe he'll change his mind. Maybe he'll come tomorrow and play.

Chapter 3
The Team

Ubly had two good left-handers in their lineup. One kid's name was Bolling and the other I forget but he had hit a shot the last time we played that had carried Solly's glove into the outfield. I remember charging the ball and seeing the glove bouncing along behind, like it was chasing the ball.

I stood next to Coach, who was filling out the lineup card. Most of the guys were throwing the ball around. Beyond the center-field fence, I could hear the rumble start, and then a whistle; the train to Chicago was coming by. Chicago was the last stop, anyway; I thought back, as it got closer, to the time Dad took Dean and me to a White Sox game. I remembered that Comiskey Park was a long way from the train station and I remembered Dean's face — as happy as I had ever seen him — when Carlton Fisk hit a three-run homer in the ninth to tie it up.

I shivered. There was a breeze, cool for summer. From behind the trees the train popped into view, sleek and dirty but still shining, with AMTRAK on the side.

Dean wasn't here yet, and it began to sink in: He wasn't coming.

"What about this brother of yours?" Coach said. I turned around. He looked up. "He gonna play or what?"

I shrugged. "I haven't seen him all day," I said. "If he says he's not playing. . . ."

He made a face and finished the lineup card. I felt bad, like it was somehow my fault. "Are you dropping Dean from the lineup?" I asked, stupidly.

"He can't play if he's not here," Coach said. He squinted at the card. He didn't look too happy with it, but he never did. "We'll put Bell in center. We'll have more power in the lineup, but we'll be about as thin as we can be. We'll be weaker up the middle, too. Your brother could field."

"Maybe he'll only miss this game," I said. "Maybe he'll come back."

"Maybe," Coach said. "But he's a stubborn kid. I haven't seen him change his mind too often. You?"

I looked down at my cleats. The orange stripes on the black were all dirty. I had to shake my head.

"What got into him?" Coach said. "You have any idea? He talk about quitting before?"

"No," I said. "He won't talk to me now, either."

"Your father talk to him?"

I shook my head.

30

He shrugged and squinted. "You know, sometimes with your brother I don't know if he's too hard on himself or too hard on everyone else." I looked up at him. "Well. If I spent too much time trying to figure out why kids do what they do — " He threw me a ball. "Let's get this deal going, then. Throw the ball around a little. Loosen up."

It was worth a try, I thought. "Do you think you could talk to him?"

He dumped out a bag of balls and bats. "If he wants to talk to me, I'll talk to him," he said. "Otherwise, if he doesn't want to play, he doesn't want to play. I'm not forcing anybody to do anything around here. That's all I need. I got enough to do with the ones who *want* to play."

I still didn't feel like going out onto the field. "Can I see the lineup card?" I said.

He handed it to me without looking. "You're still batting second," he said.

I looked at it. With or without Dean, we were still, as Herd said, monstrous. Awesome. Under ADRIAN ORIOLES, the card read:

1. Reed, Warren, ss
2. Harris, Brad, rf
3. Eades, Kenneth, lf
4. Lawler, Andrew, c
5. Robinson, Dwight, p
6. Bell, Randall, cf

7. Pearson, David, 3b
8. Ehrmann, Solomon, 1b
9. Hobbs, John, 2b

Warren was U.L. — he hated being called Warren — and he was the best leadoff man in the league. He was so tall and thin his legs seemed to go right up into his neck, and he beat out *everything* on the ground. He signed up two years ago as U.L. His real name is Warren; his hero's U.L. Washington, of the Kansas City Royals. He looks a little like him, too, especially with the toothpicks. The toothpicks drive Coach nuts. U.L. Washington, see, chews toothpicks even when he plays. Running bases, turning double plays, everything. So our U.L. does, too. He'll stand there at short, working it around from side to side, and Coach'll notice him and right in the middle of the inning he'll shout, "U.L., you got toothpicks in your mouth again?" At first he used to wait until U.L. came to the bench between innings, but U.L. had a supply in his back pocket and would pop another one in when he went back out. So now I guess Coach figures he'll embarrass him into quitting. He even mentioned it once to U.L.'s father, who doesn't come to many games: "Geez, I always worry about that son of yours with the toothpick in his mouth." U.L.'s father just looked at him. U.L.'s father is as hard to talk to as U.L. U.L. was the first black kid on the team — Kenny and Dwight came along later — and he kept to himself a lot. He was great then and he's great now. He hasn't got great hands, but he does have a great range.

I batted second. I was really ripping the cover off the ball. I was a good spray hitter, made good contact, and had good bat control. I didn't have much power but I did have some. And Dean covered for me in right.

Dean could've covered for Kenny Eades on the other side at the same time, but he never had to: Kenny could run all day and his hands were almost as good as Dean's. And he hit shots whenever he was up. He might've been the best all-around kid on the team. He kept to himself, too. I guess the black kids feel outnumbered sometimes. But he was different than U.L. He hung around with the older kids. He seemed older, somehow, even though he wasn't.

Herd batted cleanup. His real name was Andy but only his mother called him that. We called him Herd because anything hit in the dirt in front of him when he was catching was something to see — he'd fling his mask and stomp and flail around so much that he'd raise a cloud of dust that looked like the longhorns were coming through. Coach would coach him over and over to take his time, take one thing at a time, find the ball, get control of it, get set, make the throw, and Herd would nod like he understood and then go out there and stomp around like somebody being stung by bees. When he did get control of the ball, he threw it into the outfield a lot. He was a good catcher; it was just that he got so excited by balls in the dirt in front of him. Some of the guys on the bench would yell, "Stampede!" when he was doing it, which didn't help.

He thought we called him Herd because he was fat, but that wasn't it. Although he wasn't thin.

He was a real good hitter, anyway. Batting cleanup on our team, he had to be. He had the most power — six home runs up to that point — and a lot of extra bases, too, and Herd is pretty slow.

He was also probably the best friend I had on the team, after Dean. He was funny, and I appreciated that, and he was good, too, but he wasn't going to die if the team lost, like some guys. Anyway, I hung around mostly with him, or talked with him more than anyone else. Mostly, though, I hung around with Dean, and he hung around with me.

That was the thing about our team. We all got along fine but we didn't all hang around together afterward or feel we had to do anything together. I remember Kenny Eades had a party once, and someone asked him if he was inviting the team, and he said no, like they'd asked him if he was inviting someone from Montana. In that way we were like a pro team, I guess.

I realized, looking over the lineup card and not having Dean around for the first time, that I didn't see much of these guys, and didn't know them all that well, either.

Dwight batted behind Herd — he could hit, too — but if anyone would die if they lost a game, Dwight was the one. I hadn't met many black kids, and after U.L. and Kenny I thought they were all kind of cool and quiet, but Dwight straightened me out quick. He pitched, and when a line drive fell in or something got through the infield we'd hear Dwight all the way out in the outfield, groaning, carrying on. He'd drop his glove on the mound and stare at the sky until Coach would say, "Come on, Robinson, he ain't up next, the batter is." If you made an error, he'd just look at you on the bench afterward and shake his head. Let me tell you, getting a shake of the head from Dwight was worse than getting bawled out by Coach.

Randy Bell was taking Dean's place in center field, and batting sixth, even though Dean batted eighth, because Randy was a better hitter. But he was nowhere near the fielder my brother was. No one was.

Randy was worse than Dwight. He'd kill to win. He was always getting into fights. Before Dean left he thought he should have been starting in front of either of us. I didn't like him. Dean didn't like him either. He was a pretty funny guy, though,

I have to admit — someone threw a wild pitch at him once last year and after he hit the dirt he scrabbled out of the batter's box, threw his hat into the air, and ran off the field and across the street. The umpire had thought it was funny enough to let it go. But he was really sarcastic, too, and he used to call Dean and me the Amazing Two-Headed Outfielder, and used to suggest we wear the same number during games and that one of us hide in the dugout while the other either batted or played the field. I told him once I thought he hurt Dean's feelings, and he said, with this fake scared look, "Oh, *no*. Not *that*. Anything but *that*." And now here was Dean, giving him center field on the team everyone thought would be league champions.

Davey Pearson played third and batted seventh, and he was like Kenny Eades in that he kept to himself. I didn't know him real well. His parents were divorced and his little brother had been run over by a truck. I'm not kidding.

Solly Ehrmann's parents were the biggest rooters we had. Solly played first base and batted eighth and wasn't that good but was always trying, always working, always bringing questions to Coach. Everybody liked Solly. Nobody hung around with him.

Finally, John Hobbs batted last. He wasn't too bad a fielder at second, but he really couldn't hit much, and he looked it. He had round wire glasses like a Japanese sniper in a war movie and he always looked like he couldn't see anything or you were shining a light in his eyes. He and U.L. turned beautiful double plays, and I don't think they said one word to each other all year. Except maybe once, about all the chewed toothpicks U.L. was leaving around. Nobody ever called him John — it was always John Hobbs, the whole name. Nobody really talked to him much, and it never seemed to bother him.

I gave the card back to Coach and then loosened up some, stretching and jogging a bit, working up to some sprints. When Ubly was all set to go, we took the field. Dwight warmed up on the mound, and Randy and Kenny threw the ball back and forth in the outfield. They didn't throw it to me. When Dwight was ready the ump said, "Play ball!" and Kenny threw the extra ball in and turned and waited. I looked over at Randy and he looked right through me. This was the first time ever I'd been in the outfield without Dean.

The first kid popped up. Ubly wasn't real good. I could hear the coach staying after his kids, being a real pain. He was supposed to be a jerk. I knew one of the kids on Ubly and he said the coach read off who played badly after a game.

The next kid up hit a shot into the gap between right and center, and I turned and waited for Dean and realized there was no Dean, and took off after it. Randy and I reached it at the same time, at the fence, and he wrenched it away from me and threw it in. The kid went to third. He scored on a ground ball. Somebody else struck out.

We came into the dugout and Coach said, "It's all right, it's all right, it was right in the gap, let's get it back, that's all." U.L. pounded a chopper into the ground and beat it out. I came up and almost took the third baseman's arm off. Kenny hit a shot that scored U.L. and moved me to third. And Herd came up and jacked one.

We gave him a high five at home, and went over to the bench. Ubly's pitcher was crying, and the coach went out to calm him down. I couldn't blame the kid. Six pitches and he was down four to one. We were feeling pretty good.

The inning droned on. Dwight fouled off about nine straight pitches and then walked. I didn't feel so good, suddenly, and I kept thinking about Dean. I moved over and sat next to Herd.

He wasn't strapping his catcher's gear on. With Ubly he figured on a big inning.

"Nice shot," I said. He nodded. Randy Bell got a hit. Ubly's coach called time.

"You talk to Dean?" Herd said. He looked at me when I didn't answer and I shook my head.

"I can't figure it," I finally said. "I just can't figure it."

Herd was watching Davey Pearson take his

cuts. "He didn't say nothing to you?" he said.

"Nope."

Herd shrugged.

"What do you think it is, Herd?" I asked.

He looked at me strangely. "How would I know?" he said. "What do I look like, some ESP guy?"

I stared out across the field. The coach was taking the Ubly pitcher out, and he was starting to cry again.

"Do you think you could talk to him, Herd?" I said. He made a face like it was a really dumb suggestion.

I felt awful. Dean wouldn't talk to me or tell me why he wasn't on the team and nobody cared. Everybody acted like nothing was wrong.

Solly Ehrmann hit into a double play, and Herd started to strap his protectors on.

The game wasn't any fun after that. Randy didn't talk to me in center, and when we went out for the seventh inning ahead fourteen to one he said to me, "Try and catch something for a change."

Just like that. I couldn't believe it. I hadn't made any errors. I was just starting to get mad, just thinking of something to say, but it was too late. There was a crack, and I looked up and saw the ball, had a good bead on it, went forward, ran back, then lunged forward again, and it hit and sliced past me. I chased it back to the wall and Randy beat me there and threw it in. "What were you tryin' to do on that?" he said.

Dwight, rattled, walked the next two guys. The next guy up hit a liner right between Randy and me, and I hung back a second and Randy shouted, "Harris, it's yours!" and I dove sideways for it and missed, and lay in the grass watching Randy run it down. It bounced off the fence and rolled away from him. I lay there thinking, It was my ball. It was definitely my ball.

It went for a home run. Randy almost threw his arm out in frustration throwing it back in. We got them out after that, and won, fourteen to five.

I tried to avoid Coach near the bench after the game but he found me anyway and took me aside. "You know, your brother's not out there anymore," he said.

All the guys were standing around.

"I know," I said.

"You're going to have to start pulling your own weight," he said.

"I know, I know."

"Well, I'm only telling you," he said.

I smacked a bat into the bat rack, harder than I meant to.

"Listen, don't get upset with me," Coach said. "If you don't want to play right field, let me know. If you want to join your brother — "

"That's a jerky thing to say," I said. Everyone was quiet.

Coach looked at me. "You're right, it is," he said. "Sorry."

"No, I'm sorry," I said.

"Yeah, yeah, we're all sorry," Dwight said. "But we also won." He looked around the bench.

"Right on," Kenny Eades said.

"Bring on Sand Creek," U.L. said from the end of the bench, working the toothpick back and forth in his mouth, back and forth.

Chapter 4
Dad

When I got home after the game, I found a note from Mom on the kitchen table.

Dean and Brad —

Lisa and I are off to an early movie with Aunt Mina. Your father phoned and said he'd be home late, so you're on your own for supper. There are hot dogs in the freezer and fresh corn in the fridge. Why don't you just boil them both; I'd rather you didn't use the grill by yourselves.

Take care.

Love,

Mom

I put the note back. "Dean?" I hollered. "Hey, Dean!"

There was no answer.

I went upstairs and changed out of my Orioles uniform. Then I walked down to the end of the hall. Mom and Dad's room looked empty. The bed was made without a wrinkle, and Mom's desk was cleaned off. I went back up the hall to Lisa's room and pushed open the door. It was a mess in there. She'd made her bed, but then mussed it up by sitting on it all day. At least, that was what it looked like she'd done; the pillow was pulled out from under the bedspread, and the whole bed was mussed up. Albums lay all over the floor. Her stereo was still on; I went over and clicked it off. The little red light went out.

It was lonely with nobody in the house. Quiet.

I went down to the kitchen and looked in the fridge. I grabbed a Coke and some jam, then got out the peanut butter and some bread and made a peanut-butter-and-jelly sandwich. I took it and the Coke down to the play room and turned on the television.

Halfway through *M*A*S*H*, I heard a car drive up the driveway. Pretty soon the back door slammed. After a moment, somebody walked over and hollered down the stairs. "Who's that? Dean?" It was Dad.

"No! It's me, Brad." I jumped up, flicked off the TV, and ran up the stairs. "Hi, Dad. How come you're home so early?"

"It's not so early. What time is it, six-fifteen? Six-twenty?" He looked at his watch.

"Yeah, but Mom said you'd be home late."

"Well, at least I'm home, even if it's not too late."

43

He looked around. "What are you doing for supper?"

"Mom's note said hot dogs and corn. But I just had a peanut-butter-and-jelly sandwich."

"Yeah, I saw your mother's note. Are you full? Maybe I'll go out and get a bite somewhere."

"Can I go? I'm still hungry."

He looked down at me. He was wearing his suit and tie, but his tie was pulled down and his collar was unbuttoned.

"I thought you ate already. Aren't you in the middle of something?"

I could tell he didn't want to be with me. I turned away. Mom's note was still lying on the kitchen table. I went and picked it up.

"Hey, Dad," I said, "why don't we do what Mom's note says?"

"What's that? Cook our own supper, you mean?"

"Yeah. Hot dogs and corn on the cob."

"I don't really feel like cooking tonight."

"Aw, come on."

He looked at me.

"Come on," I pleaded. "I never get to see you alone. Without Dean or somebody. Can't you just stay here tonight?"

He thought it over for a second. Then he grinned. "Why not? Feel like cooking hot dogs? I'll make the corn."

"Great!"

He took off his coat and tie and draped them over one of the kitchen chairs. In no time we had coals glowing and water boiling. We shucked the corn together, and then I went outside and cooked the hot dogs on the charcoal grill. Dad boiled the corn in the big pot on the stove and put the hot-dog buns in the oven to warm. He looked funny in Mom's apron, but he wasn't lost in the kitchen at all; he knew where everything was.

We ate at the kitchen table. It was the first time we had ever eaten alone that I could remember.

I sat down while Dad put the steaming ears of corn on plates. When he put our plates down on the table, the ears rolled around and bumped into the blackened, split hot dogs. Then Dad took the pan full of buns out of the oven and put them down on a hot pad. He opened a can of Coke for me and a bottle of beer for himself. Now I had two cans of Coke in front of me.

"Where's Dean, anyway?" I asked as he sat down. "Do you know where he went this afternoon?"

"Well, not exactly."

"What do you mean, 'not exactly'?"

"Well, I mean I don't know where he went. Pass the mustard, would you? Thanks." He picked up his knife and smeared yellow mustard across the red-and-black hot dog. He took a bite.

Next he tried to butter his corn. The pat of butter kept sliding off, and he couldn't get it to stay on his knife.

"Here, Dad. Do this." I reached over and rolled his corn around in the butter on his plate.

He laughed. "Well, it's not good manners. But it works, doesn't it?"

"Sure does."

I picked up my ear of corn and ate four rows of kernels.

Dad said, "I did see your brother today, don't get me wrong. He stopped by the dealership around three. He was with some kid in a car. We talked a few minutes. I could have talked all afternoon; the place was dead today. Anyway, they drove off. Dean said something about eating supper with this kid."

"But who was he?"

"I don't know."

"Aren't you worried about him? What'd this kid look like, anyhow? What kind of car was he driving?"

"Easy, Brad, easy. Eat slow, talk slow. One question at a time. He didn't introduce him by name. He was tall — older than you and Dean, I'm pretty sure. Driving a Camaro. A red Camaro. Souped up: risers and a four-barrel, sounded like. Which reminds me, I want to put in some time on the Model A tonight." He took a swig of beer and stuffed the last third of his hot dog into his mouth.

That wasn't good manners either, but I suppose he was eating that way because Mom wasn't around. He chewed for a long time. Finally he said, "Look, don't worry so much about your brother. Maybe he's just trying to work something out. And you know Dean. He's got to work it out just one way. If we were all going down on the *Titanic*, he'd want us to use the lifeboats alphabetically."

I laughed. "His side of the room is so neat."

"And yours looks like hurricane season. Anyway, how was the game this afternoon?" he asked me.

"Lousy."

"What was the score?"

"Fourteen-five. We won."

"Good for you, son. That's great."

I hated that word *son*. Dad used it when his mind wandered off and he didn't really care whether he was talking to Dean or to me.

"My name's not 'son,' it's Brad," I said. "I'm the second one, remember?"

He chuckled. "Okay, okay. I know who you are, you don't have to remind me."

"Yes I do. Sometimes."

He reached for another hot dog and another ear of corn. He looked tired, but he ate quickly. I was full. From where I was sitting at the kitchen table I could see outside, through the screen door. Our yard bordered the one in back of us; then there was

47

another house just like ours and then the next street. The sun had set and the sky was getting dark. The streetlights were on.

I thought I heard rumbling in the distance. "Was that thunder?" I said.

"Sounds like it to me," Dad replied. "Radio said we're supposed to get a shower." He pushed his chair back from the table. "Want any more?"

"Nope. I'm stuffed. Thanks a lot."

"What's for dessert?" he asked with a grin.

"Dairy Queen?"

He looked at his watch. "Well, that's a thought. But I'd like to do some work on the Model A first. What do you say we go later?"

"Can I help?"

"Sure. Let's go."

First we piled our dishes in the sink, but then Dad said, "Whoops, let's put these in the dishwasher so your mother doesn't have to do it." We did, and then Dad went upstairs and changed into an old shirt and a pair of coveralls. We went out the screen door toward the garage. Going around the house, Dad stopped and put his nose up in the air and sniffed.

"Smell the rain?"

I sniffed the air, but I didn't notice anything different. It smelled like fresh air to me. "What rain?" I said.

"Wind smells fresh, cool. Moist."

Just then we heard some thunder. "I don't smell it, but I *hear* it," I said. He laughed.

We went into the garage through the side door. Dad flipped on the lights, and there it was, facing out, the blue Model A Ford. It had been built over fifty years ago, in 1931, but Dad had made it look brand new. Its paint gleamed, the chrome on its fenders and headlights glistened, and the windows reflected my face.

"What are you working on now?" I asked.

"I've got some work to do on the engine. Replace a part." He went to the workbench, picked up a toolbox, stuffed a rag into a back pocket of his coveralls, and walked over and set his tools down beside the car. He went and opened the main garage door. It was almost dark, and a breeze had started up.

Dad looked at the sky, then went and lifted the hood of the car. He took some wrenches out of the toolbox and began unscrewing nuts and removing bolts. I stood behind him and looked over his shoulder.

"What are you doing?"

"Well, I ordered a new part some time ago, and it just arrived. I'm putting it in."

He had loosened something, and now he removed it completely from the engine. "What's that?" I asked him.

He held it up so I could see it better. It was about

the shape and size of the cardboard in the middle of a roll of toilet paper. "This thing here is called a coil. It provides the energy for the spark, only this one is finished. See that there?"

I looked and saw only a bunch of copper wires. "What am I supposed to see?"

"It's hard to tell without something to compare it to." He reached into the toolbox and pulled out a new part that was identical to the thing he had just removed. "See this, now?"

"Oh, yeah. The new one's brighter."

"That's right. It's not tarnished. See this green stuff on the old one?"

"Yeah."

"That's corrosion. It's from moisture. After a while it just eats away at those wires, and you have to get new ones."

"Corrosion," I said. "Is that like wearing out?"

"No. Worn out is what happens to an engine part that doesn't get enough oil, or that works too hard. Wear happens to parts that move. Corrosion is different; that's when water or acid gets in and rusts parts. Corrosion occurs with parts that don't work, that don't move. They get wet and rot away."

"That's gross," I said. "I think I'd rather get worn out than corroded."

Dad gave me a kind of strange look. "Well," he said, "it's no fun to get worn out, either."

I said, "Are you getting worn out?"

He worked in silence for a while, putting the new coil into the car. There was more thunder, and at last it started to rain. The rain pattered on the garage roof, lightly at first, and then it started coming down hard. It beat on the roof and sides of the garage like a monster trying to get in. There were some flashes of lightning and more thunder, pretty close this time. But the wind was blowing from the back of the garage toward the front, so the rain didn't come in the big door.

Dad got a pair of wire cutters out of his toolbox and cut some new wires. After he had them all hooked up, he took the rag out of his back pocket and wiped his hands. "Let's crank 'er up."

He closed the toolbox and put the Model A hood down. Then he got in behind the wheel.

The car made a groaning noise, then a whirring, and finally the engine caught and roared to life. Dad gunned it a couple times, then let it idle in its funny Model A way: "Chick-a-puh-chick-a-puh-chick-a-puh."

He rolled down his window. "Hop in. Let's go for a ride."

"In the rain?"

"Sure! You can do the wipers." The Model A had old manual wipers you actually had to operate yourself. "Come on."

I ran around and jumped in the other side. Dad

51

turned on the headlights. He maneuvered around his red Mustang in the middle of the driveway, and we were off. At the stop sign at the end of our street, we headed toward the center of town.

"Where're we going? The D.Q.?"

"I want to show you something."

We drove down Main Street. The rain had let up some, but I still had to flip the windshield wipers back and forth. There weren't any people around. We went by the movie theater; it was all lit up, and it didn't look as though the first show was over yet. Puddles of rain on the street reflected the bright lights of the sign above the theater. We putt-putt-putted right through town and out the other side. Pretty soon we got to Dad's Ford dealership. I thought he was going to drive past it, but he swung into the driveway and pulled to a stop outside the door to the main showroom. He set the hand brake and sat there staring at the big windows. The headlights lit up the words on the windows and reflected off the new cars inside.

The words painted on the windows had huge letters:

BIG SALE!

FACTORY REBATES!!

ALL CARS MUST BE SOLD!!!

"Business is still pretty bad, huh Dad?" I said.

"Terrible. We'll be giving 'em away before long."

He leaned forward and rested his chin on his hands, on the steering wheel. The rain pitter-patted on the roof, and the fifty-year-old engine rocked the car as it idled in the rain. "I got into this business years and years ago, seems like. The year your sister was born. That year was like a dream, Braddy. New baby, new business — top of the world. Sure, I had worries. I didn't think a man could be in debt as deep as I was." He smiled, but he kept looking straight ahead. "Now I know you can get in much deeper."

Hearing him talk like that made me sad. "It'll be all right, Dad. Things'll get better. Won't they?"

He sighed. "They're bound to, I guess. But will they get better soon enough? That's the question." He took the brake off. "Want to go over to the lake?"

I shrugged. "Sure, I guess so."

Dad turned the car around and got back onto the highway. I worked the wipers.

I really didn't want to drive up to the lake. I wanted to go to the Dairy Queen and get home. I wondered if Dean was home yet.

But I didn't want to say no to Dad. Not tonight. He was in a strange mood, depressed and sad. I figured I'd go along with him, do what he wanted to do. It made me uncomfortable, seeing him sad like this, though. It wasn't like him. But I was still glad to be with him alone.

What Dad meant by "the lake" was the land he had bought a few years ago. It was a plot on a hill in some woods overlooking a small lake, about forty-five minutes from town. He wanted to build a new house there someday.

He drove the old Model A down the two-lane highway out toward the country. A couple of cars whizzed by going the other way, and then some guys in a Camaro passed us in our direction. They honked as they went by. Dad didn't say anything; he just drove. Dad used to race cars, but you'd never know it from the way he drove on the highway, especially in the Model A. That old original engine couldn't go very fast.

It took us a while to get to the lake, and another few minutes to climb the winding road that led up the hill. There were a few driveways and mailboxes on the way up, but they were pretty far apart. There was no mailbox at our driveway. Dad turned in and we drove through the woods and finally came to a place where a little space had been cleared. He stopped the car, turned off the headlights and motor, and opened his door.

"Are you getting out?" I said.

"I think I will."

"It's still raining." It still was, though not very hard. All Dad had on were his work shirt and coveralls, and I was wearing just a T-shirt.

"We won't melt," was all Dad said.

I followed him into the woods. The rain was falling through the trees and hitting the leaves with loud slapping sounds. Big cold drops of water hit me on my back and shoulders. We stepped over logs and around trees, and sometimes brushed against wet bushes. Most of the time we were walking uphill. It was dark, but not pitch-dark; we could see where we were going. Finally we came out on a kind of ledge; the woods ended and the hill dropped away almost straight down. Right in front of us was the lake. We were quite a ways above it, but we could hear the rain hitting the water.

This was the exact spot where Dad wanted to build our new house. From up here we could see a long way. Off toward the horizon were the lights of town. There was a car going down the old highway; you could hear its wheels on the rainy pavement and see its headlights. And just below us, now, as my eyes adjusted to the dark, I could see the lake. The wind was blowing, and gusts of wind and rain swept the lake. Sheets of water were rushing across it. They looked like huge waves. It was a small lake, but the rain on it at night looked beautiful. I could see why he wanted to build a house up here.

The rain started to blow into my face, and I was getting cold. I turned to say something to Dad, but he wasn't there.

"Dad?" I said. "Where are you?"

I turned around and took a couple steps and then I stopped. He was just a few feet away, sitting on a log. His shoulders were slumped, and he was hanging his head. He looked small — smaller than he'd seemed to me before. He looked like Dean after he struck out.

I walked up behind him and hugged him — put my arms around his shoulders and my head on the back of his neck. His neck used to be so big. Now it wasn't much bigger than my neck. It smelled like him, like a mixture of the smell of his and Mom's bedroom, and the gas-and-tire smell of the Ford dealership.

Droplets of rain dripped off Dad's hair and nose. His face was wet. But he was very warm, and it felt good to lean on him like that. The side of me that was getting rained on was very cold.

Pretty soon he patted me on the top of the head and got up. We started walking back to the car.

"I don't know if I'll be able to keep this," he said. "If business doesn't pick up soon, I won't be able to make the payments. I'll have to sell it."

"Aw, don't worry about it," I reassured him. "There's nothing wrong with our old house. We all like it plenty."

We got back to the car and climbed in. Dad kicked the starter. It turned over with its groaning noise, but the engine wouldn't catch. Dad tried it over and over, but it wouldn't start.

"Did I put the toolbox in the back?" he said. He got out and opened the back door. "Nope. No tools, no flashlight. Great."

He shut the door, walked around to the front, and lifted the hood. He bent over the engine and began fiddling with things in the dark.

I watched him from the front seat. I had my arms wrapped around myself to try to keep warm. If we had to walk home in this weather, we were going to freeze.

He worked away for a few minutes. Finally he climbed back in behind the wheel and turned the key. He kicked the starter and she started right up.

"All right!" I said. Dad gunned the engine and it backfired, breaking the stillness of the woods. "Way to go, Dad! You're magic!"

"Not really. You'll learn that soon enough." He got out and closed the hood. Then he climbed back in and swung the car around toward the road. He said, "You'll learn that soon enough, Brad. I'm just another car salesman."

Back at the house, Mom's car and the Mustang were blocking the driveway. By this time Dad and I were freezing because the Model A had no heater.

"Go on inside and jump in the shower," Dad said to me. "I'll put this antique away."

I went inside while Dad started moving cars

around. I ran straight upstairs to our room. Dean was lying on the bed, reading some book by Ted Williams. He put the book down and looked at me. "Where've you been? You're soaking wet."

"Where've *you* been?" I started taking off my clothes.

"Never mind."

I shrugged. "Dad and I went for a ride out to the lake. He says he might have to sell it. Whose car were you driving around in this afternoon?"

"Just this kid. Why's Dad going to sell the lake?"

"He doesn't want to. Business is slow. So what's going on with you, anyway?" I was standing there in my towel, shivering.

"Why don't you go take your shower? You look purple."

"What'd you do this afternoon? Tell me!"

"No." He picked up the book again.

"You know, you're really being great," I said. "Thanks a lot." I slammed the door. A picture fell off the wall with a crash, but I didn't care.

Chapter 5
Coach

Coach asked me just what, precisely, I thought I was doing out there. I told him I had been trying to stop the run from scoring.

He looked down at his shoes, then up at me, and then down the bench. "Trying to stop the run from scoring," he said.

I looked over at Dwight. He shook his head.

In the previous inning I had fumbled a line drive hit right to me and then had overthrown the cut-off man, trying to gun the runner out at the plate myself. I'd missed the runner by enough to make it look like a pretty stupid idea.

We were playing Sand Creek and were now down one to nothing because of me. "Let's go, guys," Coach called as U.L. stepped up to the plate. "Big rally. Just like Ubly."

U.L. lined out. I grabbed a bat and hurried to the plate. "Let's go, Harris," Coach called. "Get it back."

I wanted to. Too much. I overswung, and beat this thing into the ground that Lisa could have

59

thrown me out with. Kenny flew out to the outfield.

"It's all right, it's all right," Coach said as we were heading back onto the field. "Don't let up on defense. Hold 'em here." Randy snickered, jogging out next to me. I could've belted him.

The inning went quick. Kenny made a nice shoestring catch, and Davey Pearson threw somebody out from deep in the hole. We came back up and went down almost as quick, getting a couple guys on base before Solly made the last out. He came back to the bench and thumped it with his fist. "It's okay, Solly," I said.

"No, it isn't," he said. "It was low and outside."

"Shake it off," I said.

"I stink," Solly said. He grabbed his glove and took the field.

With a guy on second, Sand Creek's catcher hit a looping line drive to center that Randy charged, trying to shoestring it.

I stood watching him like an idiot until I heard Coach yell, "Brad, back him up!" right before the ball skipped by him. I was so late chasing it that Kenny beat me to the ball from way over in left. Two to nothing.

I stood near the bench, watching John Hobbs take some practice swings. Coach came by and huddled us all together. "If we get some kind of decent lead on these guys I want to juggle some positions around," he said. "Fremont has a guy here scouting us. I don't want him to find out anything they can use." I looked over at the bleachers. A bald guy was sitting alone, nonchalant. Fremont was the best team in the league besides us, and we played them at the end of the season. We looked at him, excited by the idea of somebody scouting us.

John Hobbs led off and got a hit. U.L. and I looked at each other. "Far out," U.L. said. He stepped in, fouled off a pitch, and got a hit himself.

I stepped in. "C'mon there, Brad good-eye, good-eye kid." I took a ball high and outside. "Good-eye, good-eye kid." I drove the next pitch deep into the gap between right and center, and as I motored around the bases I thought, If that kid's anything like me as a fielder, I'll score for sure.

He wasn't. He got the ball into the infield pretty well, and I slid into third and almost overslid. Our bench was up, cheering. I stood up, and whacked the dirt off my legs.

They stranded me there, and we didn't even threaten again until the fifth. With the score still two to two I came up with Davey on third and U.L. on first and pounded one down the line. Standing on second I could see U.L. getting the high five after scoring and I thought, Okay. They can blame me for two runs. And they can thank me for four.

I was still thinking along those lines when we took the field for the top of the sixth, so I got what I deserved. Sand Creek's leadoff man sliced one over second and Randy and I both charged it hard and I saw him at the last second, a blur in my peripheral vision, and I managed to turn my head away just as we collided. My head snapped back and I bounced on the grass like a rag doll. I lay there mixed up for a second, my mind moving slowly, and got up on one elbow. The kid was scoring. Randy was limping a little after the ball, without his hat or glove, but it was Kenny who finally ran it down, from over in left, and threw it in.

Everyone made sure we were all right, and I guess we were.

The scout from Fremont was looking over at us. I thought, What're you looking at, jerk? The next kid up hit a fly ball toward me and I overshot it, stopped, and fell back for it and missed. I held the guy to a single. Dwight was looking at me, his glove on the mound next to him. Randy was muttering in center. And Sand Creek's coach called his batter back from the on-deck circle, and huddled with him. He pointed at me.

I felt like my stomach drained away. I knew, suddenly, that they knew about me. I backed up a step in the outfield, almost as though I could get away. Kenny was looking at me, too. And Coach. My forehead was cool. I realized I was sweating. The kid got into the batter's box and slowly closed his stance, turned it to face right field a little more.

I knew what they were doing and my hand shook, once, before the kid connected and drove one in front of me for a base hit. It got by me and Randy stopped it, backing me up.

The next kid up stepped in with a closed stance, too. "Oh, no," Randy said in a low voice. "They're on to it." I wanted to signal Coach, stop the game, do something. I couldn't do anything. The kid hit one on the ground, and Solly made the play unassisted.

A left-hander came up. Oh, Lord, I thought. On the first pitch he rocketed one down the line and I couldn't get to it, running, running, and diving, letting myself hit as hard as I could in frustration once I realized I wasn't going to reach it. By the time Randy got to it it was a triple, and the two runners had scored, and we were behind five to four.

Oh, Lord, I kept thinking. Get me out of here. Somebody, get me out of here.

The next kid up was left-handed, too. He hit a real shot foul, and then another foul, too. Coach was almost out on the field, waving us over, shifting Kenny and Randy toward me. Kenny was playing practically in center: The whole left side was open. And the kid still was swinging for me.

He ended up walking. Dwight was circling the mound, talking to himself. Then he threw a wild pitch and the runner went to second. Coach came out to talk to him. He settled him down, somehow: Dwight threw a strike, and then a ball that just missed. The kid got under the next pitch and hit a high foul to right, way off the field, and I ran for it but couldn't reach it. From the infield it must've looked like it dropped right through my glove. I came back to the field feeling naked, alone. Everyone was looking at me. The kid hit the next pitch with everything he had. It was right over me and I was ahead of Randy in getting to the fence. I kept thinking, *Oh, get it, get it, get this one*, and I jumped at the fence and mistimed it, coming back down as the ball went over. Randy screamed. Solly turned around, and Dwight fell to his knees. I almost got up and left right then and there.

After somebody grounded out I came back to the bench last, feeling like I'd never felt before, hating myself for playing this way. The bald guy from Fremont watched me go by.

I led off the seventh, the last inning. I struck out. I couldn't believe it. I stood there, staring at the bat, and the umpire finally said quietly, "Come on, son." I sat at the end of the bench still holding the bat, and I think I was starting to cry for the first time ever on a baseball field. We were behind seven to four and I was responsible for all seven runs. I'd lost this game all by myself.

The season was over and it was my fault.

I tried to cheer when Kenny singled, but I

couldn't. Herd wound up and hit one out, over the center-field fence, and our bench was jumping up and down, and I managed to smile and wipe my eyes. I hoped they could win and I wanted to say, hey, you guys deserve better than me. Dwight got a hit, too, and everyone was shaking their fists and pounding the bench. I started to think maybe we could do it.

Randy flied out, and threw his bat. The umpire almost threw him out of the game. He retrieved it and carried it very gently in front of him, like a finished jigsaw puzzle, back to the dugout.

"Come on, Davey, need it, Davey, let's go," Coach called. Davey hit a slow one toward third and the whole bench was up as he tore down the line. When he beat the throw we let out a yell my parents probably heard at home.

"Come on, Solly," Coach called. "Come on, Solly," his mother called from the bleachers. "Come on!" Solly swung and missed it by a foot. "Wait for your pitch, Solly," Coach called, "wait for your pitch." Solly looked over. Coach gave him a take sign. Solly looked at him and turned away. I felt sorry for him, but Coach probably had to do it. Solly was in such a slump. He waited with his bat cocked, took a ball, another strike, and three more balls and tossed his bat aside without looking back and trotted to first.

It was up to John Hobbs. He squinted and

picked out a bat and went up and dug himself a little spot in the batter's box and hit one over the second baseman's head to win the game.

We mobbed him. We couldn't believe it. He'd never gotten two hits in a game the whole year. He didn't look surprised at all. Just another routine game-winning hit for John Hobbs, batting .198 with one extra-base hit.

We celebrated for a while and then just sat around, exhausted. Some of the guys were getting rides home, or walking, and some were still hanging around, not wanting the moment to end. I sat down at the end of the bench, happy for everybody. Dwight and Herd were still slapping each other five. John Hobbs dawdled around, edging his bike back and forth. Kenny Eades gave him a soul shake on the way past and Herd whooped and shook him by the shoulder.

Coach reminded them about Fremont and practice, and John Hobbs trailed off after Dwight and Herd, leaving us alone. Coach went around the bench picking things up. He looked tired and you could hear his breath when he bent over. I watched him collect the baseballs and bases and I suddenly felt bad that he had to do everything so I got up and started getting the bats together. We brought everything to his station wagon and piled it in.

"C'mon, I'll give you a ride home," he said.

"I can walk," I said.

"I know you can walk. You can sing, too, but there's no reason to. Get in."

We got in and he pulled out into traffic.

"We're not gonna be so lucky next time," he said.

"I'm sorry," I said. "I'm so lousy out there."

"That's not what I meant." He tapped his fingers on the wheel, waiting for the car in front of him. "C'mon, dear, it's only a stop sign," he said. He turned to me. "You're not lousy out there."

"I am. I stink."

"You got no confidence, that's all. You're playing some of those line drives like they were grenades."

"You shouldn't play me against Fremont," I said, looking out the window. "The guy was onto me today. They'll kill me."

He stared straight ahead, the way he looked at the lineup cards. "We're thin enough without your brother," he said. "That's number one. Number two, we can use your bat. And number three, we don't give up. Do we? We can work with you. I can work with you." He looked off to the left and back to the road.

I stared out my window. "If only we could get Dean back," I said.

"We don't have him," Coach said. "And we're not going to fall apart without him. We got somebody who can play center. Now all we have to do is make sure you can play right. At least enough to get by."

We swung onto my street, and I looked at my

house up ahead. Dad was washing the Mustang in the driveway. "I still wish he was back," I said.

"Brad, you're gonna want to become a complete ballplayer someday anyway," he said.

I rolled my window up and down a little. "It's not that," I said. "It's not that. I don't even care if he doesn't play. I just want him around."

We pulled up in front of the house and my father waved. Coach honked the horn and waved.

"He hasn't been talking to you at all, huh?" Coach said.

I shook my head.

He made a sympathetic face. I looked over at my father, who was looking up every now and then to see what was going on.

"He's older, Brad," Coach said.

"I know he's older. Everyone tells me that. He was older before."

"I'll try and talk to him," Coach said. "Tell him I'd like to see him. Ask him to come talk to me."

I thanked him.

"Look, how about this," he said. "Tomorrow I'll meet you at the field and we can work on your fielding. And see if you can get Dean to come along, and I'll talk to him."

I thanked him again and got out of the car and he drove off with another beep for my father. When I came up the driveway Dad said, "What was that all about? Strategy?"

"Yeah, I guess so," I said.

I told Dean at dinner that Coach wanted to talk to him, and that it wasn't just about getting back on the team, and that I was throwing the ball around with Coach tomorrow, so he could meet him then.

At first Dean didn't answer and Dad said, "If Coach wants to talk to you, you should talk to the man," and so Dean said yeah, and I said we'd go over around four and he said he'd meet us there, he had something to do, and that was the end of that.

When I showed up at four the next afternoon, Dean wasn't there yet.

"All right, well, let's go," Coach said. "We got some things to do anyway." I went out to the outfield and he hit balls to me. After a few, he called me in.

"You're waiting too long on them," he said. "You shouldn't move on them until you know you've judged them right, but you should be able to judge them faster than you're doing. You got good speed and good coordination and good hands and you're crippling yourself. It's like everything's coming out of the lights, or something."

He hit a few more out to me. One of the ones that got by me went all the way back to the fence.

"Concentrate on it," he called. "It's just a matter of judging it."

I walked the ball back in. "I just never had to do it before, I guess," I said.

"It's okay. Now's as good a time to learn as any."

I misplayed another one and, as I turned to walk after it, I noticed Dean across the street, sitting on a fence on the corner. He was wearing white and he stuck out against the green of the lawn behind him. I waved him over. He didn't move. I threw the ball in. "Dean's over there," I said.

"I see him," Coach said. "Let's work on first things first."

I walked back farther into the outfield and he hit a wicked line drive over me that I just sort of stabbed my glove at like an idiot and missed. I walked after the ball with Dean, on the fence, watching me.

He hit another solid shot and I went way back, running hard, trying to judge my leap, and jumped. It ticked off the webbing and bounced against the fence. I bounced off the fence myself and threw my glove at it. Dean didn't move.

I came back into the infield. "I give up," I said.

"What do you think you're going to get out of one day of work?" Coach said. "Circus catches?"

I sat on the bench. "I guess you're right," I said. "I'll come out here a couple of times before the Fremont game."

Coach put the bat down. He waved to Dean. "Call your brother," he said, but Dean got up and headed over.

Coach sat on the bench next to me, and we both watched Dean walk up. He stopped a few feet away, his hands in his pockets. Coach twirled the bat end in the dirt.

"Hiya, champ," he said. "Long time no see."

Dean smiled a little. Coach twirled his bat.

"I hear you guys had a great comeback against Sand Creek," Dean said.

"Umm-hmm," Coach said.

Dean looked around, sort of uncomfortable.

"Listen, Dean," Coach said. "I know I said this wasn't just to ask you back to the team, and we're doing all right, but we sure could use you in center. You're the best fielder in the league and Randy and Brad are doing a good job, but you don't replace the best."

"I can't play," Dean said.

"Listen, if it's something I said, or something —" Coach said.

"No. It's nothing."

"What about your brother here? What's the deal with him? He says you barely talk to him now."

Dean looked at me and I felt like a fool suddenly. I gave him a sheepish look, and he said, still looking at me, "I talk to him."

Coach scratched his neck, watching Dean. "Dean, it's none of my business, but if there's something bothering you — something you don't want

71

to talk to your parents about — "

"No." Dean kept his eye on the end of the bat.

Coach stood up. "Well, I don't know what your brother's upset about then," he said.

Dean shrugged. "We don't hang around much together anymore. We're doing different stuff."

I looked at Dean. He looked back evenly. I couldn't believe it. And Coach seemed satisfied. I wanted to say to both of them, Hey, that isn't enough! But I could see they were both ready to end this.

"Well, you keep us in mind," Coach said. "You can always come back. Here's the good news: I never officially dropped you from the team." He headed for the car and turned. "You guys want a ride?" We both shook our heads. "You can walk back together, I guess," he said. He got in the car and drove off, waving once. We watched him go.

"Want to go to the movies tonight?" I said.

"I don't know. Maybe," Dean said. "I gotta go somewhere. See you later."

I watched him cross the street and move down it on the other side, past the fence he'd been sitting on.

It was quiet on the diamond except for a car now and then, and I made a little telescope with my hand and watched my brother's back bob along the sidewalk against the hedges, his white shirt catching the sun before disappearing around the corner.

Chapter 6
Herd

And then I thought: Why don't I follow him and see where he's going?

I picked my bat off the ground and grabbed my glove from the bench, and I took off after Dean.

Maybe he was going to meet that kid with the Camaro!

I ran across the diamond and crossed the street. A block ahead of me, he disappeared around the corner, heading away from our house. I hurried down the sidewalk after him, my plastic spikes clicking on the concrete. Overhead the trees formed a canopy across the street, and their leaves rustled in the evening breeze. The noise of the leaves was like bedclothes. On the other side of the street, a woman stuck her head out her screen door and called her cat: "Heeeerrrre, kitty-kitty-kitty-kitty!"

I meowed. She gave me a dirty look, slammed the screen door, and disappeared inside her house.

I laughed, almost out loud. My heart was thumping inside my chest. This was exciting.

At the intersection I looked up the street. Dean was nowhere in sight. I started running. I kept looking both ways, first right, then left, and just past the next street I saw him heading across somebody's backyard. I ducked behind a tree and watched as he walked between two houses and disappeared from view.

Now he was going roughly in the direction of our house. Was he going home?

The lawn I had to cross had just been mowed; it smelled good and felt soft under my spikes. I peeked around the corner of the house and I saw him, still walking fast, about a block away, just about to cross a street. He paused, looked both ways, then trotted across the street, and swung up onto the sidewalk.

What the heck? I thought. He's just heading home.

I jogged along through people's backyards. Some of the houses had televisions on in the kitchen, and there was a family eating in one of the houses. The parents and kids were gathered around the kitchen table, and I heard one kid say, "Oh shut up. You don't know what you're talking about." Farther on, a couple of dogs barked at me, and I passed a grill that had a whole chicken turning on a spit. It smelled great.

When I reached the sidewalk I slowed down and just walked along. Dean was more than a block ahead of me; he'd see me if he turned around, but I didn't care. Let him. He was walking home the long way 'round; I was sure of that now.

I thought about tomorrow. We had a day off with no baseball. I didn't have any plans and didn't know what I was going to do. Maybe play some ball. I needed the practice. But who'd work out with me? Before, when I wanted to play ball, I'd just get out my glove and go find Dean. By the time we got out to the park, he'd feel more like playing. He'd pitch and I'd hit, or else I'd just hit him flies. It never really worked the other way around. I always wanted to hit, and he wanted to throw and play the field. We never traded off much; we just did the thing we liked best.

Up the street, Dean turned the corner toward our house. He was two blocks ahead.

When we were little we didn't just play baseball. We played stickball, too. We'd go over to the high school and play against the big brick wall around back, in the parking lot. We'd have a supply of eight or ten tennis balls, and I'd use a sawed-off piece of an old hockey stick for a bat. Dean would pitch, and I'd hit. All the batters were me, but I'd be somebody different each time up: Cal Ripken or Alan Trammel, Reggie Jackson or Lance Parrish. I batted lefty and righty; it didn't matter. We'd keep count on each batter. That was how I learned to fight off pitches when I had two strikes on me; that was how Dean learned to throw hard and to field hot line drives and fly balls.

In those days I liked stickball better than baseball. We'd play for hours.

I took my spikes off at the back door, put my gear in the closet, and went upstairs. I didn't know what exactly to say to Dean, but I sure wanted to find out where he'd been all day.

He wasn't in our room. I checked the bathroom, then went back downstairs. He wasn't in the kitchen or the living room, so I went down to the basement. He wasn't in the TV room either.

I went back up to the second floor, breathing hard. I checked our room again, then knocked on Lisa's door. Nobody answered, so I looked in. No Dean, just the usual mess: new clothes and old records all over the place.

Mom was down in her room. She was dressed up in some exercise outfit — tights and a purple thing that looked like a bathing suit — and she was lying on the floor doing sort of leg-lifts.

"Mom?" I knocked on the door frame.

She looked up at me. "Hi."

"What are you doing?"

"Yoga. I started yoga classes this week. Remember?"

"Oh yeah. I didn't think it was like this, though. Aren't you supposed to sit still? Think about your navel or something?"

"Very funny. It's really just exercise, mostly stretching."

"Oh. Hey, did Dean come home?"

"Haven't seen him," she grunted. She let go of one leg and grabbed the other.

"You sure?" I said. "I thought he would've come home a few minutes ago."

"Of course I'm sure," she said. "Leave me alone now, would you, Brad? Be a dear and shut the door. Thanks."

I closed the door.

He gave me the slip, I thought. He must have known I was following him. He didn't come home at all.

I decided I wouldn't speak to him that evening. Not a bit, not a word. And I didn't.

Because he didn't come home.

At least, not until breakfast. At breakfast, when Mom and Dad and Lisa and I were sitting around the kitchen table, he walked in the back door, poured himself a bowl of cereal, and sat down as though nothing had happened. Mom and Dad knew where he had spent the night, even though they weren't supposed to tell me; I'd learned that much the night before. So now, at breakfast, I tried to play it cool. If Dean could act as though nothing unusual was going on, then so could I.

Dad said, "Hi, Dean. Have a nice time?"

"Sure," said Dean.

Dad nodded. He was reading the paper. He said to Mom, "Did you see these new unemployment figures?"

"No, dear. I haven't read the paper yet."

"It's terrible."

"It'll get better. Don't get excited."

"I'm not getting excited!" Dad said, louder than he probably meant to. I looked at him, surprised, and so did Dean and Lisa. Mom looked at him, too. "I'm not getting excited," Dad said, softer. "I'm just remarking on the news, that's all."

"What are you doing today, Dean?" I said.

He chewed and swallowed. "I don't know. I'm busy around three."

"Want to play some stickball?"

He leaned back in his chair. He appeared to be thinking it over.

"Maybe," he said. "Where? Over at the high school?"

"Yeah. Where else?"

"I don't know." He took a bite of cereal, then said with his mouth full: "Want to pitch?"

"That wouldn't be any fun."

"Maybe it would."

"Are you kidding?" I couldn't believe it. "You can't hit for beans, and I can't pitch any better than Lisa."

"Watch it," said Lisa.

"All right," Dean said, "forget it. We're too old

for stickball anyhow."

I realized I'd just blown it. But this strange kid sitting across the table was so unlike Dean, so different. Usually all I had to do was mention stickball or catch and he'd be out the door. And often it was his idea.

"No, that's okay," I said, hoping it wasn't too late. "I'll pitch. Let's play after breakfast."

He shrugged and kept eating. "Forget it. When's the next Little League game?"

"Tomorrow. You don't want to play stickball?"

"No thanks."

"You going to play in the game?"

"I don't think so."

"You mean you might?"

"No. No way."

I could just barely control my temper. I felt like smashing him again. I got up and dumped the rest of my eggs in the garbage, rinsed my plate off, and put it in the dishwasher. I walked out of the kitchen.

He hung around the house most of the morning, reading on his bed or doing something at his desk. After lunch he said something to Mom, got his bike out of the garage, and left.

I got my bike out too and took off after him.

I was a little stiff from all the running the day before. Dean rode pretty fast, over to the park, and across the railroad tracks. Then he headed toward the center of town. I waited at the park until he was just about out of sight, and then I followed. I stayed a good distance behind — three or four blocks — but I saw him look back a couple of times, and I knew it was no good. If I could see him, he could see me.

Just about that time a car alongside me slowed down. The driver beeped his horn, and when I looked over, I almost fell off my bike.

It was the red Camaro.

The driver was a blond-haired kid wearing a T-shirt. He was tan and looked pretty strong. He grinned at me, and waved.

"See you at three?" he yelled.

He'd mistaken me for Dean. I thought fast. "Where?" I shouted.

"Same place!" he yelled. "Three o'clock." I saw him shift the car into gear, and then, with a roar, he patched out.

The noise of his tires accelerating almost immediately blended into the sound of his brakes squealing. He brought the car to a halt ahead of me, opposite Dean. I saw Dean lay his bike on the sidewalk and go over to the car window to say something.

I started pedaling, fast. But just as I almost got there, the car took off again. Dean turned and faced me.

I put on a burst of speed, then slammed on my

brakes, and laid a rubber strip five yards long. I nearly rammed him but he didn't flinch.

"Kids' games," he said. He stood on the sidewalk with his arms crossed.

"Who is that?" I demanded.

"None of your business. When are you going to quit playing games, anyway?"

"You're the one always sneaking off."

"Don't be juvenile. And quit following me."

"I'm not following you. I'm just out for a ride."

"Bull. Look, I know you followed me yesterday. That's why I went home. You can't follow me without me knowing, and I'm not going anywhere as long as you're following. So just quit it. Go do something else and leave me alone."

"Dean," I said, "what's the matter with you, anyway? Is something wrong?"

"No. Now bug off."

I looked him in the eye, and I could tell he was serious. He just didn't want me with him. That's what was so weird; this was not the kid I used to have so much fun with. I wanted to say something to him, say the right thing. I wanted to tell him how he used to be so much fun to be with, and now he wasn't, but I still wanted to be with him, even though he didn't want me. I felt like asking him where the other Dean was, the one who used to play stickball with me for hours.

But that Dean was gone, and I didn't think this

Dean knew where to find him. "All right," I said. I wasn't angry anymore, just sad. "You go on. I won't follow you again."

He picked up his bike and straddled it. He looked at me and I thought he was about to say something else, but he changed his mind and just said, "See ya," and pedaled away.

I watched him go. After he was out of sight, I looked around. I was standing in front of a big house on the corner of Main and Third. There wasn't anybody around, so I laid my bike on the lawn and sat down on the grass.

I was feeling sorry for myself and I didn't know what to do.

But I did know one thing: I was tired of being alone. Who could I go see?

Third and Main, I said to myself. Herd lives near here. Yeah, Herd lives on Third.

I started pedaling up Third Street.

It didn't take me long to get to Herd's. He lived in a big house that was halfway up the hill. There were some steps that went up to a porch, and I carried my bike up and rang the bell.

Herd opened the door.

"Hi," I said. I didn't know what else to say.

"Hey, Brad! What are you doing here?"

"Nothing," I said. "Just passing by. What are you doing?"

"Oh, I was reading."

"Yeah? What were you reading?"

"I don't know. Some book." Herd was a big kid with freckles and a dirty face. He had brown hair that covered his ears, and his voice was hoarse, probably because of his asthma. He breathed loudly, too. "Want to do something?"

"Yeah."

"What?" he asked.

"I don't know. Play some catch?"

"Got your glove?"

"No."

He gave me a funny look. I felt sort of stupid.

"I've got a couple extra. Come on in." He opened the door wider. I'd been in his house a long time before, and I didn't remember it too well. It was big, and the furniture looked old. All the chairs and stuff had been made a long time ago, most of it. Antique. I liked it, but it seemed kind of dark. The windows were small, and the furniture was dark blue or dark green, and the wood tables and chairs were all very dark, too.

"Is anyone else home?" I asked.

"No," he said. "Mom's at work."

I followed him through the living room and kitchen, then down a hallway to a small room in back, where he kept all his sports gear. He opened the door and we went in. There were hockey skates and football shoulder pads and a lacrosse stick and tons of other junk thrown every which way around the room. It was all goalie's gear: a goalie's lacrosse stick, a goalie's skates and hockey stick, and a catcher's mask and shin guards and chest protector. The whole floor was covered with sports equipment, that's all there was — cleats, bats, jerseys, sticks, sneakers, hats, helmets, balls, gloves, and pucks — no bed, no bureau. It was a whole room of sports equipment, all for one kid.

Herd waded into it and dug around underneath some stuff and pulled out a catcher's mitt and a couple of old gloves. "Here, pick one," he said, and I chose the bigger of the two gloves, a dark brown one, stiff, with a couple of laces broken. Herd fished around and found a baseball. Then we went out the back door to a level area in front of the garage. It was bright out there and I had to squint. He flipped me the ball. We started a game of catch.

"We gonna kill 'em tomorrow?" he hollered.

I grinned. "You know it!" I rifled a throw at him that almost sailed clear over his outstretched mitt. He had to jump for it.

A serious look crossed his face. "Your brother playin'?"

"I don't think so."

"How come?"

"I don't know. And it looks like I'll be the last one to find out. I don't think Dean's ever playing ball again."

"Oh yeah, he will. Someday."

"Maybe. Not this season."

Herd held the ball in his hand for a moment, and tossed it up and down. He said, "You want me to hit you some? I've got a bat. We could ride down to the park."

"No," I said. "Let's just play catch." I was still sore from chasing those fly balls Coach had hit me. Still humiliated, too.

"You sure?"

"Yeah! Come on, throw the ball."

So we played catch for a while. The glove he loaned me loosened up in the heat, and it didn't feel too bad.

Every time he threw, he grunted, and he threw hard.

I made some low, backhand catches and fired the ball sidearm like an infielder.

"Nice throw!" he said, catching the ball like a first baseman. He threw me pop-ups and grounders, and I caught them, too.

A while later, he stopped throwing and walked over. "This is boring. Let's get something to drink and sit on the porch."

We went inside. Herd poured iced tea from a pitcher in the fridge and added sugar and lemon and ice. We went outside and sat on the front steps. We could see Third Street and a white house right across from us, and down the hill we saw the green treetops and the tarred roofs of the three-story buildings along Main.

I sipped my tea slowly and tried to make it last.

"Hey, Herd," I said, "how'd you ever get to be the catcher, anyway?" Then I thought about it, and realized I shouldn't have asked. The slower kids always get stuck with those positions.

"I don't know. Why?"

"I was just wondering."

Herd drank some iced tea and wiped his mouth with his bare forearm. He said, "I guess it was Pop, actually. Pop always wanted me to be a catcher, and a goalie. He was always the goalie when he was a kid."

"What does he do, anyway? Your father, I mean."

Herd gave me a funny look. "He's dead," he said, and looked away from me. "He died about five years ago."

I almost choked on my iced tea. "Oh yeah," I said. That was the time I saw his home last, after the funeral. "I remember. I'm sorry."

"That's okay. It's not your fault." He laughed. "I don't know. Pop just went out and bought me a catcher's mitt and all that other crap. I didn't like catching. I still don't. I'm not crazy about foul tips. I didn't like playing goalie, either, not in hockey or lacrosse, but that didn't matter to Pop. If you were good at it, not liking it wasn't an excuse not to do it.

86

Anyway, when he — "

He stopped talking. He looked out at the trees for a second, then continued. "When he had his accident, well, I figured if he wanted me to play goalie, I'd play goalie. And catcher."

"What if Coach wanted you to play some other position?"

"I guess I'd do it. If there was a good reason for it."

I nodded. Then I said, "I never heard you talk about your dad before."

"No. I don't like to talk about him. You never asked about him before, either."

I folded the fingers of the glove backward. "What happened to him, anyway? Wasn't he fishing or something?"

"Sailing. He drowned. It was windy and he tipped over and he wasn't wearing his life jacket."

"Couldn't he swim?"

"Yeah. They think he had a heart attack, too. But they're not sure."

"That's too bad, Herd."

"I don't really remember it much. But he did used to play a lot of ball with me."

"Your mom makes men's underwear, doesn't she?"

He looked embarrassed. "She *designs* men's underwear, she doesn't *make* it. There's a difference, you know."

"Yeah, I know. That's a good job, isn't it?"

"It's all right. She makes enough money, that's mainly why she does it. And there was some insurance, so we're not poor or anything."

"You're lucky," I said. "My dad's got business problems. Anyway, I like your house. It's really nice."

"Thanks. So do I. There's tons of room. You ought to come over and spend the night sometime."

"That'd be fun. I'd like that. Would you want to invite Dean over, too?"

"I don't know. Do you two always do everything together?"

"Well, we used to, pretty much. Not lately, though."

"He could come if he wanted. But I was just inviting you. I don't know him very well."

"Me neither. At least, not anymore, I don't."

Herd laughed.

"Hey, Herd," I said, "do you know some guy who drives a Camaro? A red Camaro? I've seen Dean talking to this guy, and I don't know who he is. Dean won't tell me."

"Red Camaro?"

"Yeah."

"How old a guy?"

"I don't know. Seventeen, eighteen maybe."

"Sounds bad."

"What do you mean?"

"Well," he said, setting down his glass, "if he's only seventeen and owns a Camaro, chances are he sells pot or something."

"Get serious," I said.

"I am. How many seventeen-year-olds do you know who can afford a Camaro?"

"I don't know *any* seventeen-year-olds."

"Well, Dean does. Probably a drug dealer or something. You better watch out. Your brother could be in a lot of trouble."

"He's never smoked pot that I know about." That was a lie. "Well, once, maybe, but not around here. That was at camp, when we were real little."

"I don't like the sound of it. What's this kid look like?"

"He's blond. A big kid. I don't know, I couldn't really tell. He was in the car." I suddenly remembered something. "Wait a minute. Dad met him. Dean stopped by the dealership a couple days ago and introduced him. He wouldn't have done that if the guy was a druggie, would he?"

"Sure he would! That's all the more reason. Heck, I'd introduce him, too. That way, nobody'd get suspicious. Those drug dealers are that way — real smooth. They can snow anybody."

Herd was making me feel worse and worse. I didn't think he was right, but what if he was? Was Dean into drugs? He didn't seem spaced out or anything — just distant. Changed. Unfriendly.

Maybe it *was* drugs.

"See you at three."
"Where?"
"Same place."

"Let's go look for them!" I said suddenly. I jumped up and went over to my bike.

"Who?"

"Dean was supposed to meet him someplace. That kid in the Camaro. Let's go see if we can find them."

Herd gave me a disgusted look. "How are we going to do that?"

"I don't know. We'll ride around. Get your bike."

Herd stayed put. "They could be anywhere."

"There's two of us. We can cover a lot of ground."

"Brad. Think about it. The kid's got a *car*."

"So?"

"They could be miles from here. They could be in Fremont. It'd take us an hour and a half to get to Fremont."

He was right. I sat back down.

"Anyway, don't worry about it. Dean's got to learn to take care of himself. Besides, we've got better things to worry about. We've got a game tomorrow."

"Big deal. We can't beat Fremont without Dean."

"Yeah. Right," Herd said. I knew he was being sarcastic.

"With me and that jerk Bell in the outfield? No way. They scouted the Sand Creek game."

"Look, Brad, I hate to tell you, but we can get along fine without your precious older brother. Why's this eating at you so bad, anyway? It's no big deal. Forget it. We can win games with or without the great Dean Harris. Sooner you learn that, the sooner you'll begin to play some defense out there." He was getting red in the face. He paused to take a couple of deep, rasping breaths. "Nobody's indispensable, you know what I mean? We can win without Dwight's pitching or my catching or your hitting or Dean's fielding. You watch. You wait and see tomorrow."

"That's what I'm worried about. Tomorrow. My fielding."

"You oughta be."

I got up and picked up my bike. "Thanks, you fat head."

"Hey." Herd got up and stuck his hands in his pockets. "I didn't mean it the way it sounded. I just meant you could play better, that's all. Better than you did against Sand Creek."

"No kidding."

"Well you *can*. There's no law against learning to play the outfield. You could work on it."

I nodded.

"It'd help the team. Why don't you practice or something?"

"I did, yesterday. Coach hit me some flies."

"Did it help?"

"I don't think I got any better."

"It takes time to get better. Baseball isn't easy."

I thought about it. The game against Fremont was tomorrow, and I'd been chasing Dean around for two days instead of practicing.

I looked at Herd. "How late is it?" I asked him.

He checked his watch. "Four-thirty."

"Listen," I said. "How about if we hit a few around? I'll go get my glove."

"Am I hearing right?" He tipped his head and hit it with the heel of his hand as though he was knocking water out of his ear. "*You* want to practice?"

"Shut up. Get a bat and some balls. Meet me at the park."

"All right!" Herd was grinning. He looked up at the sky. "Plenty of daylight left," he said. "We can practice for hours."

Chapter 7
Mom and Dad

T he Fremont Pirates were already in the field warming up. Six or seven big kids roamed the outfield in their black-and-yellow uniforms, shagging flies, and they had nine guys taking infield practice. They had more subs than we had players.

I went over to our bench. Most of our guys were there.

"Who've we got here?" U.L. said. "Let me see that glove. Left hand. You're the one that hits, ain't you?"

I saw Herd down the bench. "How's the hand?" I asked him. He'd hit to me the day before until he had to quit because of blisters.

"The hand's fine," he said. "It's the asthma I'm worried about." His face was a strange shade of pink.

"You'll make it," I said. "Probably go four for four."

Someone shouted: "Hey, Orioles! Heads up!" Coach was walking over from the parking lot, and he'd lobbed a ball toward us. It hit near the bench.

He was carrying his equipment bag. "Get ready for batting practice. Let's go, hustle!"

Coach wasn't the only one heading over. The parking lot was jammed, and cars were still pulling in. People were hurrying toward the diamond, carrying picnic baskets and thermos jugs, the men wearing sunglasses and caps, the women in wide-brimmed hats. Both the Adrian and the Fremont stands were already more than half full. I couldn't believe how many people had come to watch the game.

Then again, maybe I could believe it. After all, this was the championship game. If we won, we'd win the league and be in the playoffs.

Pretty soon Fremont finished their warm-ups, and we took the field. We rotated around between fielding and batting practice. I was the third one to hit. The stands were nearly full; I could hear a buzz when I stepped up to the plate, actually hear people talking about me in the stands.

I took a few swings at the junk Coach threw me, sending the ball rocketing toward Eades in left, shooting it past Coach toward center, and then knocking some line drives to right. There was a little less noise all of a sudden from the Fremont side, and that made me feel good. Then Coach threw me a fastball right down the middle and I relaxed and stroked it and the ball disappeared over the left-field fence. Applause from our stands. I bunted three or four slow curves, and that was it.

Feeling cocky, I looked over at the Fremont stands, and the first person I laid eyes on was the bald-headed guy who'd been at the Sand Creek game. He was staring at me. When he saw that I recognized him, he grinned a nasty grin, and then he looked at the sky with his mouth open and held up his hand like he was trying to catch a fly ball, but was going to miss. I went back to the bench for my glove and walked out to right field. He'd spoiled it for me.

I looked up at our stands to see if Mom and Dad were there yet. They had promised they'd come, and if they did, it'd be the first game they would both see this season. Each of them had been to one or two games alone, but not together. I had been excited about their both being there, but now I wasn't so sure anymore. What if I blew it the way I had against Sand Creek?

Then I saw them, walking in front of the bleachers looking for seats. I waved, but they didn't see me. Dean wasn't with them.

I walked out to right field. "Hey, Harris!" Randy shouted at me. He threw me a ball. I caught it and threw it back. We warmed up our arms, and then he threw me some high ones. I didn't have much trouble with them, though I lost one in the sun. When our warm-ups were over, Coach called the team in from the field and told us to sit down on the bench. It took him a minute to get everybody seated and quiet. He said he wanted to talk to us, and everyone finally shut up.

Coach said, "Okay, listen up now. We don't have much time. You've got to be on the field in" — he checked his watch — "exactly three minutes. Now look. I've said it all before, I'll say it again. You can beat this team. You know you can. You know what you got to do. You got to hustle, you got to think, you got to stay awake out there, concentrate. But I want to say one thing more. This is the game for the championship. Whoever wins this game — you or Fremont — they're league champions. You'll go on to the playoffs if you win this one. The district playoffs. But here's what I want to say. This could be the last game of our season. There's no shame in that — everybody's season ends with a loss. Except Taiwan, usually." A couple of guys got the joke and laughed. Coach continued. "The rest is gravy. Win this one and you've got a lot of fun ahead of you. The playoffs. But you've had a great season anyway. You've worked hard, learned a lot, won a lot. And that's how it should be. If we get into the playoffs, we'll have fun. You'll see some sharp players then — but you've seen good players all season. You've got no one to be afraid of. You're good baseball players. So whatever happens out there today, play your best, relax, stay on your toes, and remember: Win or lose, it's been a heck of a fine season. Seemed like a short season, though — I wish it could last forever. But it doesn't. It's gone before you can blink.

"Okay, let's go!" He clapped his hands. "Let's go get 'em!"

We took the field and the game started.

Fremont had clearly gotten the word from the jerk who'd scouted the Sand Creek game. Their lineup was loaded with left-handers. The first kid up grounded out to John Hobbs, and the next kid was a righty, but he tried to hit it to me anyway. He popped up to Dwight, and I thought, Serves you right, creep. The next guy up was another lefty, and he didn't swing till Dwight had two strikes on him. But when he swung, he *swung*! And connected. It was a low, hard line drive to my right, and I started after it as fast as I could go. I didn't think I could catch it. I ran toward deep center, but I stayed away from the wall, figuring to play the bounce. Randy Bell dived at the ball and missed (Dean would have had it easily), and the ball bounced off the grass and skipped over the fence.

Ground rule double.

I went over to give Randy a hand up.

"Where were you?" he said, slapping at the dirt on his knees and elbows. "That was your ball."

I'd taken enough. "Did you hear me call it?" I said.

"No."

"Then it wasn't my ball. Why didn't you catch it? We're standing in center field."

He looked around and didn't argue.

The next batter was their clean-up hitter, another lefty. Dwight worked hard trying to strike him out. He worked him to a full count, but then he walked him.

Men on first and second, two out.

A righty stepped to the plate, and I relaxed a little. Coach waved me in shallower.

The batter faked a bunt on the first pitch and took strike one. The next pitch was a ball. He swung at the third pitch and hit a short fly ball over John Hobbs' head. I hesitated before I started in after it. It came right at me but it was short, and I ran as hard as I could. At the last moment it seemed to loop to my left. I ran past it going in the wrong direction.

I stopped, turned around, and chased it into foul territory. I couldn't hear Solly or John Hobbs for all the screaming in the stands, so I didn't know where to throw. I picked the ball up and threw home. I knew it wouldn't be a long throw, and I knew it should arrive on one bounce. It got there in two. Blocking the plate, Herd backhanded my throw beautifully and went sprawling as the baserunner barreled into him.

He lay there in the dust for a second, and then

weakly raised his mitt. I could see the ball in it.

The umpire signaled "out," and the inning was over.

Herd limped over to the bench and sat there wheezing noisily. "You okay?" I asked him. He only nodded.

I had a chance to talk to Coach.

"What should I have done on that first one?" I asked him. "I was going to play it off the wall."

"That was fine, fine," he said. "But the last one — slow down a little as you get near the ball. Be ready to go sideways. Keep the ball in front of you."

"Sorry."

"Hey." He patted my arm. "Nice throw. You got him by a mile."

I went and got my bat and started thinking about hitting.

U.L. got on, and when I came up to bat, the guy in the booth behind the backstop announced my name over the loudspeaker. This was such an important game that they'd put in some kind of P.A. system, and it was scary to hear: "Now batting: Brad . . . Harris!" The sound echoed off the trees and houses surrounding the field. I felt good. I dug a hole in the batter's box with my spikes and wondered whether I could crank one my first time up.

But Coach gave me the bunt sign. I took a ball and a strike, then bunted toward first. The catcher fielded it and hit me in the back with the ball. U.L. went to third, but their first baseman ran the ball down and threw me out at second. A few moments later, Kenny's long fly brought U.L. home with the first run of the game.

Herd hit a grounder and was thrown out by a mile, and Dwight popped up, so we went into the second leading by a run.

On my way out to right field, I looked up in the stands. I picked out Dad and Mom, but they weren't paying much attention. Dad was talking to some guy sitting next to him — he looked familiar — and Mom was reading a book.

Reading a book! Why come to the game at all if she was going to sit there and read a book?

The next inning was mostly infield play, although Kenny Eades made one spectacular catch. He chased a foul ball way over beyond the bleachers and just did get to it, but the ump said the ball was out of play. No one argued; it was our home field, and we probably knew the ground rules better than the ump. Most of us had been playing there for years. But it was a matter of principle to Kenny, I guess. He had a play on the ball, and he made it. That made me think.

We didn't score in the second, but they did in the top of the third. One of their lefties came up with men on first and third and one out, and hit the ball hard between Solly and John Hobbs. As the ball came bouncing toward me I charged it, and then I got down and blocked it. I almost fielded it cleanly, but it popped out of my glove. I picked it up and threw to John Hobbs, who fired to Solly. The batter, who had thoughts of going to second, had to dive back to the bag, and we thought we got him. But the umpire called him safe.

In the meantime, the man on third scored easily.

The next batter hit a sharp single to Randy, who charged it and threw it in so quickly that their third-base coach held up the lead runner at second. It was a nice play, and I saw the whole thing from directly behind him because I ran over to back him up. When he turned around after the play and spotted me behind him, he looked surprised.

"How'd you get over here so fast?" he exclaimed.

"Mirrors," I said. "What's the matter? You think you don't need backing up? Nice throw."

Dwight struck out the next hitter, and we were out of the inning. They'd tied it up, one to one.

That was the last run either team gave up till the fifth. In the fifth, their first two batters were righties; it looked like they'd given up on the idea of hitting to me. Too many of them had popped up. Now they seemed intent on just hitting the ball. Their second baseman hit a sharp grounder to Davey Pearson at third, and Davey bobbled it just long enough to allow the guy to beat the throw. He kicked the dirt. The scorer gave the Fremont kid a hit. Next, their catcher got a bloop single to left. So after throwing about four pitches, Dwight was in trouble. Men on first and second, nobody out.

The next batter, a left-handed first baseman, hit a sharp grounder to second. John Hobbs and U.L. turned two, and we were back in good shape. Two outs, man on third.

The P.A. system announced their number nine hitter, the shortstop. He was right-handed. Somehow that kid hadn't gotten the word, because he was swinging for right all the way. He got lucky. He hit the third pitch and he got all of it. It soared fairly high and right toward me, not a fly ball really, but a high liner, and I stood there, not wanting to move till I was sure I had to. It seemed to be coming right toward me. I put up my glove, but then suddenly the ball was fading toward my left. I took two steps toward the foul line and stretched my hand way out, and the ball sailed past me and on into the corner.

I chased the ball, my feet heavy as lead, my heart thumping, wishing I could relive that moment, wishing I could jump the fence and keep running, wishing I were anywhere just then but there. By the time I'd picked up the ball and thrown to John Hobbs, who relayed to U.L., the run had scored and the batter was standing on third.

I felt awful. But something was dawning on me, too.

That ball had curved.

I'd never thought of a fly ball or a line drive as a curve before. I'd thought only pitches curved. But as I stood there in right field, my hands on my knees, my heart racing, breathing hard and waiting for the next batter to settle into the batter's box, I replayed in my imagination the two balls I'd missed that day. I'd misjudged them both, not for distance, but for their right-to-left movement. They'd both been hit by righties, and they'd both curved from my right to my left.

Maybe I'd learned something.

And maybe that was what made it look so easy when Dean did it, charging from center field the way he used to do. When he came over from center to catch a fly ball in my territory, he was running in the right direction. The ball would be curving away from him, so he'd just speed up and run it down. But if I moved *in* toward a ball that seemed to be coming straight at me, it could curve out of my reach toward the foul line.

Maybe that was why I'd missed so many. I'd never played a ball to curve before.

The kid on third didn't score. The next batter overswung and popped up to Herd, who seemed to feel better. He caught it way over by the bench and made it look easy.

I didn't bat in the fifth. I was glad, because I wanted some time to calm down and think things over. Nobody talked to me on the bench; we were down by a run, two to one, and it was my fault. Nobody even looked at me.

At one point, I turned around and looked for Mom and Dad in the bleachers. They were there, all right. The man sitting next to Dad was jawing away at him. Mom had put down her book; she was leaning forward and talking to the woman sitting in front of her. I turned around three or four times, hoping to catch their eye, but neither of them was paying attention to the game. They didn't look at me once. I could have been dead, for all they knew.

It occurred to me that maybe they didn't want to be there. It occurred to me that they could go on living their lives perfectly happily whether we won or lost this game. They had lives of their own, and friends of their own, and this game probably wasn't very important to them.

Thinking all that made me feel pretty depressed.

But the game was important to *me*. I got my mind back on baseball.

As we took the field in the top of the sixth, I caught a couple of glances from Dwight and Kenny Eades. I wanted to tell them not to worry, but that would have been foolish. They wouldn't have understood.

I got one fielding chance in the sixth. It was a high, short fly ball that Randy got a good start on. He parked himself under it while I trotted over to back him up. Suddenly I saw him look away and cover his eyes with his bare hand.

"Sun!" he shouted.

I'd never seen that happen before. I don't think Dean ever lost a ball in the sun.

The ball was coming down fast and I scrambled for it and at the last second I dived. I caught it and slammed into the ground hard, and the ball rolled away from me.

Eades picked it up and threw it to U.L., holding the hitter to a single.

"Good try, Brad," John Hobbs hollered.

"Stay with it," Eades said over his shoulder as he walked back to left. "Don't let up now."

I wasn't about to let up. We held them to no runs that inning, despite the dropped fly, and we went to bat in the bottom of the sixth still down by one run.

I led off. I didn't look up at my parents as I selected my bat and loosened up in the on-deck circle; I didn't want to know that they weren't watching. When I stepped up to the plate, all I wanted to do was get a hit. Preferably extra bases.

Coach called time and started over, and I met him halfway to first.

"He was starting to get wild in the last inning,"

Coach said, speaking of their pitcher. "Take a few pitches, see if he walks you."

I almost said, "I want to hit it," but I kept my mouth shut. I knew Coach was right; Eades and Herd and Dwight all followed me in the line-up.

Coach seemed to be in the habit of being right. Maybe that was why we listened to him. The pitcher threw two straight balls, both way outside, and when I stepped out of the batter's box, Coach was frantically waving the "take" sign at me. I watched a slow fastball nick the corner for a strike, and I mean "nick"; I wouldn't have swung at it anyway. The next pitch was low, and Coach still had the "take" sign on, and sure enough, the next one was ball four.

Big deal. I hadn't swung the bat once.

Eades came up next and sacrificed me to second. Herd swung away and popped up; he flung his bat as he left the batter's box, and the ump called him out for poor sportsmanship while the ball was still in the air. I thought I was going to be stranded on second, but Dwight walked and Randy hit a solid single to left. I got a good jump because there were two outs and I was running on anything, and I came home standing up with the tying run. I was greeted with a lot of cheering and hand-slapping; nobody cared whether I'd gotten a hit or a walk, the run counted just the same. Davey Pearson, up next, hit a squibber that the second baseman bobbled, and Randy rounded second and headed for third, running for all he was worth. Their bench started shouting at the second baseman to throw to third, *THIRD!*, and he did, sending the ball sailing over the leaping third-baseman's glove. I didn't want to look at that second baseman after that; I knew too well how he felt. Randy scored, of course, and Davey went to second. Solly drove Davey in with a shot up the middle that glanced off the pitching rubber and bounced into left field. That was all, though; they changed pitchers, and the new kid struck out John Hobbs on four pitches.

So we took the field leading by two, four to two. It was the top of the seventh, maybe their last ups. If we could hold them for one more inning, we'd be the league champions.

A train went by and I missed the P.A. announcement about who was batting first, but it was a lefty. Dwight worked him to a two-two count, and then he hit a shot on the ground past Solly along the foul line. I got over just in time to stab at it with my glove; I picked it up and threw it to John Hobbs. He threw too high to U.L., and the kid slid into second with a lead-off double.

The next guy up, another lefty, hit a smash at Dwight. Dwight reached out, caught the ball cleanly, whirled and threw to second for the double play. Only there was nobody on second but the Fremont Pirate. The ball bounded into center field, and the baserunner tagged up and took off for third. Randy's throw wasn't even close.

They had a man on third with one out, and we had only a two-run lead.

Their next batter, the second baseman, hit a hard line drive down the left field line that landed foul. On the next pitch, Dwight hit him in the small of the back.

Men on first and third, still only one out.

Their catcher was up next, another righty. He fouled off three pitches, all in my direction, and I tensed up. Coach waved me in a few steps. When he finally hit it fair, it was high and deep, a fly ball, not a pop fly. I back-pedaled under it and waited. The ball hung there, a dark speck against the blue sky; it seemed to float forever. It started down, and I didn't wait. I moved to my left a few steps, then a few more steps, my eyes glued on that ball, waiting for it to do something strange like curve. Maybe it was curving, but I'd played it right. It grew larger and finally *whapped* into my glove.

I pulled it out and threw as hard as I could. Solly cut it off and threw home. The runner from third slid in while Herd was still waiting for the ball. My throw wouldn't have got him, but I'd finally hit a cut-off man.

Four to three. Man on first.

The next batter was their new pitcher, a strong right-hander, and he hit a grounder up the middle that Dwight and John Hobbs both missed. Randy charged in to scoop it up, and the ball rolled cleanly between his legs. I picked it up and threw it to U.L. on one hop, and he held the runners at first and third.

Randy's face was red, and he didn't look me in the eye. "Nice play," he said sort of sullenly.

The next batter was their first baseman, and Dwight walked him on five pitches. Bases loaded, two outs. Top of the seventh. The people in the stands were going crazy.

Coach went out to the mound. Dwight listened, strangely calm. He shrugged a couple of times, and finally nodded. Coach returned to the bench.

Their shortstop grounded out to our shortstop, and the game was over.

We were league champions.

Dwight leaped about a mile off the mound, and Herd threw off his catcher's mask and ran toward him. Then all the players converged on them. I was one of the last; I leaped onto the pile and started pounding everybody in sight. We rolled around in the dust until we were exhausted and filthy, and then we started sorting ourselves out.

I found my cap and glove and walked toward the bench. I felt fantastic. I had my arms raised over my head and a huge grin on my face. League champions! It felt great. The best team for miles.

Back at the bench, we were all laughing and

shouting.

We gave Fremont a cheer and shook hands. I finally picked up my bat and walked over to the bleachers to find Mom and Dad. Dean might be around somewhere, too, I thought. I waded through the crowd, still wearing this huge grin, and people patted me on the back.

"Nice game, son."

"Way to go."

Dad was off to one side of the bleachers talking to the guy he'd been sitting with. I walked up and he didn't look at me, so I went off to find Mom. She was over talking to her lady-friend.

"Hi, Mom."

She broke off her conversation. "Ready to go, Brad?"

"We won! We're league champions!"

"Good for you, Braddy." She smiled at me. "I knew you could do it. You played very well. Now why don't you go find your father, and we can leave."

I walked back over to Dad, wondering if I had a disease of some kind.

This time Dad saw me coming. "Brad! Come here and meet somebody. Brad, this is Mr. Frank Baird. Mr. Baird, my second son, Brad. He's number two, but he tries harder."

"Pleased to meet you, Brad."

We shook hands. "Nice meeting you, Mr. Baird.

Did you see the game?"

"Sure did, son. Heck of a game. Went down to the wire. Say, you had some problems in right field, didn't you? What was it? Sun bothering you?"

"No." I didn't say anything more.

Mr. Baird looked at my father.

"Brad, talk to him," Dad said. "He doesn't know about your fielding. You looked better today."

"Thanks," I said. I couldn't believe they could ruin something so fast. "Can we go now?"

"Is your mother ready?"

"She's waiting for you."

"Okay. You go and find her. I'll be right there."

I turned to go.

"Say good-bye to Mr. Baird," Dad said.

"Good-bye, Mr. Baird. Nice meeting you."

"Same here, son."

But I didn't go back to where Mom was standing, still talking to her friend. I looked around for Herd, but in the crowd I couldn't find him. Maybe he'd left already. I wanted to get away, so I started home by myself. I wanted to enjoy the way I felt and I didn't want to be around anybody who'd spoil it for me.

I wanted to take this feeling, this confidence, all the way to the playoffs.

I'd worry about Dean, and about Dad and Mom, some other time.

Chapter 8
Lisa

Lisa had the stereo up loud. Dean was out. I wandered back and forth from the window to the bed in my room, not knowing what to do next. If I felt so bad I had to have a real problem, but if nobody thought I had a real problem, maybe I shouldn't feel so bad. That's really bright, I thought. You're making progress.

I knelt by the window, my chin on my hand on the sill. Lisa played the Beatles, or other old English groups. They had to be old, and they had to be English. The music came right through the wall: *"I'd like to be / under the sea / in an octopus's garden, in the shade."* Dumb song, I thought. I felt crabby. "I'd like to be under the sea, too," I said. "Anywhere but here."

I looked over at Dean's desk. He'd left a half-finished bag of M&M's, the open end rolled up neatly, under the lamp. I spilled some out and arranged them in three precise rows on the desktop, alongside his pencils. I sat back down. I thought about what Herd had said. Maybe I should go through his stuff, I thought. I went over to his dresser and opened his bottom drawer and poked around in the back, behind some shirts he never wore. If I was going to hide something, I figured, that's where I'd hide it. But then I stopped looking, and slammed the drawer shut. What was I going to do if I found something? And who cared, anyway?

I sat with my back to the wall, legs straight out. The stereo went off. I stared at a spot on the floor and scratched my leg. Lisa went by the door. After a minute she poked her head in.

"What's the matter?" she said.

I sat up a little, surprised. "Nothing," I said. "Where you going?"

"Going out with Sue," she said.

"You didn't make yourself up like that for Sue."

She laughed. "No, I didn't."

"Is what's his name going to be there? Bob?"

"Rob. Don't be nosy. Oh, gosh, I don't have a towel." She turned away from the doorway and opened the linen closet. She pulled out a big towel that had FLORIDA written on it and stuffed it into a straw bag she had everything in. "Here, check this out," she said. She took a pair of sunglasses and set them up on her head, in her hair. "What do you think?"

I looked at her, wagging my foot. She was real pretty. I always sort of knew that, as a brother, but it hit me now in a different way. She had beautiful brown hair that was straight and full and curled under. She had really nice eyes. She had put some kind of lipstick on that shone a little and was almost the color of her lips, and it made her look older. She had very smooth skin. "My beautiful clear-skinned Lisa," Mom always said, and I guess I was beginning to see what she was talking about.

"Well?" Lisa looked at her leg. She wasn't fat at all, but always thought she was. I thought she was too skinny, myself.

"You look eighteen," I said.

She smiled and got a better grip on the wicker bag. "Gosh! I'm going to ask you more often!" she said, and said good-bye going down the stairs two at a time.

It was funny. I could be all depressed and then something could happen like that with somebody like Lisa, who I never talk to even, and I'd feel better.

I don't mean I never actually talked to Lisa; we got along and everything. But she was an older sister, and to her we were little kids most of the time, and I was even littler than Dean. We didn't particularly want to hang around a lot with a girl, anyway. And she was always playing her stereo and she just talked about and worried about completely different things than we did. Mom and Dad treated her differently, too.

Anyway, I felt good, sitting there like a three-year-old, still looking at my feet, feeling good because Lisa had poked her head back in. Then the same thought hit me about Lisa that I'd had earlier about the team when I had been looking at the lineup card: I really didn't know her very well. I tried to think about what I knew, what I was sure of, tried to pull my memories of her together, and I felt like I had missed or forgotten everything. I felt awful suddenly; I felt like an idiot. It was just like Dean, just like the team: I didn't know anyone, really. The more I thought about it, the worse I felt. I started to get more frustrated thinking about how easily Lisa had made me feel better and how quickly I'd felt rotten again, and I thought, Are you some kind of nut? I shook my head and pictured myself sitting on the floor like a fool, worrying about all of this. If someone had said to me, Brad, what's wrong with you, what would I have been able to say? Nothing, I guess. I'm just being stupid.

Dean clomped up the stairs and came into the room. He tossed a book he was carrying on the desk and went over and sat on the edge of the bed. He started untying his shoes. "What're you doing on the floor?" he finally said.

"Nothing," I said, watching him.

He looked over at me. "Okay," he said. "I'll buy that."

He opened a dresser drawer and I fought an urge to ask him where he was going.

He pulled out a bathing suit and flipped it behind him onto the bed. He lifted a leg and took off a sock, and looked over at me again. I was still sitting there, legs out. He took the sock off the other leg and dropped his pants. He stepped out of them and kicked them into the laundry pile. I looked over at his bathing suit: a green-and-white Speedo. We'd seen the high school swim team last winter and we'd both wanted Speedos really bad after that. Mom had finally given in about a month ago, when we'd dragged her into Herman's to show her the sale. I think they were seven dollars. Dean had gotten the green-and-white and I'd gotten red-and-white, same patterns.

He dropped his underwear and shook his thighs to help them slide down, then stepped out of them and into his Speedo. It went over his rear with an elastic snap. He pulled his shirt off and grabbed one from the dresser drawer that said THIS IS LION'S COUNTRY, and pulled it over his head. He left the room and I heard the linen closet door open. "No towels," he said to himself. He came back in, pulled his sandals out from under the bed, and put them on.

Have a good time at the beach, I wanted to say. Don't drown. I didn't say anything.

He checked the linen closet once more before clumping back down the stairs.

I went over to the window after a second and

watched him pick his bike up off the grass. He got on and pedaled down the street, and I turned away before he was out of sight.

He still wasn't back by dinnertime. Lisa came in, out of breath, her hair sticking out at a funny angle from the beach. Mom told her to use a towel if she had to sit around in her wet bathing suit. We all sat down and Dad poured himself a beer. I wasn't going to ask; if nobody else wanted to know, neither did I. Mom passed around a dish of sliced cucumber and fennel. Lisa commented on the fish. We all sat there, eating.

"Where's Dean?" Dad finally asked.

"He went sailing," Mom said. "He said he'd probably be back late."

I put my glass down.

"Sailing?" Dad said. "With who?"

"Billy Kletter. He got a new sunfish, I guess."

"Billy Kletter has his own boat, huh?" Dad speared some fish with his fork and looked over at me. "How come you didn't go?"

Mom shushed him. I finished my fish and went upstairs.

It was cool out. I sat near the window and looked down the street. It had been such a beautiful day. It got dark so much earlier now, I thought.

I heard someone pad up the stairs, and my door squeaked open.

Lisa stuck her head in. "How about a

man-to-man talk?" she said.

"You're a sister," I said.

"Well, I guess that's the end of that idea." She sat on the edge of the bed. "You want to talk anyway?"

I shrugged, not sure what she meant. Lisa never did things like this.

She stood up. "I'm going to listen to some records," she said. "You want to play some?"

"Maybe I will," I said. "Thanks."

"Well. I'll be in there. I'm going to shower first. You can put something on if you want." She tossed her old towel on my laundry pile and left.

I stayed by the window, rubbing my arms as it got colder. The sun was starting to set and the orange glow came all the way down the street along the sidewalks, on the road. Lisa was singing in the shower. It pretty much drowned her out, but every now and then she'd rise above it. It went off and I could hear her humming and finally she padded into her room. The stereo went on. She left her door open.

I paced away from the window and sat by the desk. I didn't recognize the group. I listened some more, and I still didn't know who it was. I flopped down on the bed but almost immediately I thought, this is stupid sitting here by myself, so I went into the hall, and looked around, and finally poked my head into Lisa's room.

She was sitting on the bed, in shorts and a

football shirt. She looked up and smiled. I stepped in and sort of stood there, not knowing what to say. "I think your room's cooler," I said finally.

She nodded. "I'm on the corner," she said. "Even when Mom makes me shut the door because of the music, I get a breeze."

I leaned against the door jamb, rubbing my palm on my elbow. I felt weird. "Who's that?" I said, motioning toward the stereo.

"The Yardbirds," she said. We were quiet again, listening to the songs. They were noisy, with a lot of guitar, but I began to like it after a while. I looked over at Lisa. She was reading the liner notes on the album. She didn't look at all uncomfortable. I felt better. I looked around her room. Everywhere I looked were things I'd never seen before, or never really noticed: some weird pieces of driftwood, some shells arranged around a plant in the corner, a cork bulletin board with *Go Adrian!* buttons on it, pictures of horses, and a picture of Lisa with her arms around Dean and me on vacation last summer. We were all grinning.

"You want to hear the other side?" Lisa said.

"Sure."

She reached over without getting off the bed and flipped the record over.

"Who are the Yardbirds?" I said.

She held up the record cover. I went over and sat next to her, on the floor, and looked at it.

"They were really a great group," she said. "You know Jeff Beck, Jimmy Page, and Eric Clapton were all in it?"

"Really?" I said. I wasn't sure who they were.

"You know who they are, don't you?"

I started to nod, but then I smiled, and shook my head.

She smiled back. "Page is the lead guitarist for Led Zeppelin. Jeff Beck's been in a lot of bands and Eric Clapton's been in Cream, Derek and the Dominos — "

"Yeah, I know who Eric Clapton is," I said. I looked at the album cover again. They really must have been some group, I thought. All those guys at the same time.

Lisa leaned over and pointed out a picture of the three of them together.

"'Course, they weren't all in the group at the same time," she said. "Wouldn't *that* have been something?"

I agreed it would've.

"They really inspired a lot of groups," she said. "They did a lot of stuff first that a lot of groups still do now."

I looked at the picture, and then up at her. "How did you hear about them?" I said.

She reached over and moved a hair away from my eye.

"Rob's older brother," she said. "He showed

Rob. Rob showed me. And now I'm showing you."

"Thanks," I said. "That's neat." We sat there, just listening. We'd never done anything like this before, it seemed to me.

"Dean's really bothering you, huh?" she said.

I looked up, surprised, and looked back down again. "Umm-hmm."

"Is it because he doesn't hang around with you anymore? It's not just that he quit the team."

"No, it's not that. At first I just wanted him to play because I was so bad and I was scared playing without him, but I'm getting better, and even if I wasn't, it wouldn't be that. It's just all of a sudden he doesn't like me."

Lisa was quiet and it dawned on me sitting there that that was it. In a way, it was as simple as that. My brother didn't like me.

"Oh, that's not it," Lisa finally said, quietly.

"Yeah, it is. He just doesn't want to see me anymore. He doesn't talk to me, he won't do anything with me. Like today he went sailing. He never asked me."

The stereo was off. It was almost dark out. We could hear crickets.

"I just want to know what I did," I said. "I just want to know why he's mad at me or what's wrong."

"He *is* older, Brad," she said.

"I know," I said. "And I'm younger. He's also

121

taller, too. And I'm faster."

"Well, maybe his ideas are changing. Things he wants to do are changing. You'll feel the same way."

"How much older is he?" I said. "Everyone makes him sound a hundred-and-fifty. He's not older than you. You don't ignore me. Suddenly he's a grown-up and I'm a kid?"

"No, Brad. I don't know. I'm just saying you should be a little patient."

"He shouldn't treat me this way. He's always been older, and he shouldn't treat me this way." I played with the album cover.

"Well—" She stopped, thinking. A moth hit the window screen next to her. "He may not be mad at you at all. And maybe nothing's wrong."

I looked at my hands, and blinked. "All he'd have to do is say that," I said, really quietly.

The crickets went on for a little while. "Remember vacation last year, Brad?" she said finally. "Remember the three of us went sailing and beachcombed up the beach and found all those floats that had washed ashore?" I nodded. "Well, it's like we had a lot of fun, but I don't do that with you guys now." I thought of the picture on the bulletin board. "I don't go sailing or hang around with you guys. And it doesn't mean I'm mad at you or anything's wrong. It doesn't mean I don't love you and everything."

I sat listening to the crickets and the other sounds outside. The breeze was cold on my back.

"I guess it's just that Dean was always my best friend," I said. "I don't even have that many other friends."

Lisa ran her hand along the edge of the bed, smoothing the light bedspread. "It may just be that Dean thinks he has to do this, Brad. You know, like in a way he needs room or something."

"I don't know. I don't take people's room, do I?"

She gave me a little smile.

"I mean, how come he needs room and I don't?"

"How come you can hit and Dean can field?"

She smiled down at me again, after a minute, and then I smiled, too.

"Am I going to need room in eleven months?" I asked.

"Oh, Brad, I don't even want to think about it," she said.

I felt better, even if I wasn't exactly sure why. I was sure Lisa had something to do with it, though, and I felt grateful. I wanted to hug her.

"Aren't you doing anything tonight?" I said.

"I'm supposed to go over to Sue's — she's having a pool party."

"When?"

"Seven."

I looked at the clock. "It's seven-thirty," I said.

She shrugged. "I'll be a little late." She got off

the bed. "Let's go," she said. "I'm going to change into my new suit. No free shows."

I got up, leaned the record jacket against the stereo, and went over to the door. "Lise?"

She rummaged in the drawer. "Uh-huh?"

"Thanks for everything. Thanks for being so nice."

She smiled, blushing a little. "Just remember the next time you see Rob: I look eighteen."

I shut the door behind me so she could change.

I went downstairs and Dad was in the kitchen, squeezing lemon into some iced tea.

"Your sister plays music that would wake the dead," he said.

"Those are the Yardbirds," I said. "They're real good."

He looked at me.

"They had Jeff Beck, Jimmy Page, and Eric Clapton all in the same band. And they did a lot of things other groups copied later."

He was still looking, lemon dripping into the tea. "Oh, no," he said. "That's all we need." He dropped the lemon into the glass with a plunk. "Another one. Wouldn't that be just perfect?"

"Not a lot of people know about them," I said.

He looked back once more before taking the glass into the living room. "Wouldn't that be just perfect?" I heard him ask Mom. "Another one. Wouldn't that be just perfect?"

Chapter 9
Me

L ight was streaming in my bedroom window and Dad was standing over my bed. Dean was gone and his bed was made.

"What is it?" I said. "What's up?" I was still sort of asleep.

"I thought we'd head out and take a look at the lot," he said.

"Okay. Now?" I sat up. Today was the game. "What time is it?"

Dad laughed. "Not now. Come get some breakfast first. I wanted to get started early."

He went downstairs and I got up, still a little disoriented. I went over to the window and stood near the screen to see how warm a day it was. I was cool, standing there in my underwear. Maybe it would warm up.

I put on my shorts and high basketball socks, wondering. What was going on? Dad seemed like he was in such a good mood. And we never just went "to take a look at the lot," except that one time a few days ago. We usually went to cut firewood or clear brush or spread gravel on the road in. I pulled on an old Adrian uniform top and thumped downstairs, carrying my sneakers. I sat at the kitchen table and put them on. Dad was at the stove.

"We're all out of juice," he said. "There's coffee there."

I took the pot off the warming tray and poured myself some. "Where's Mom?"

"Went shopping. Today's the sidewalk sale at the mall, so all the nuts are out in force by nine. If you don't get there early, there's nothing left but hangers." He looked over at me for the first time. "That's some outfit."

I looked down. There was a big ORIOLES across the front of me in orange and black against the white, and the shirttail hung out and over and almost covered my green shorts. My basketball socks had big dark blue and yellow stripes. It did look weird.

"Well, you don't have to worry about hunters with an outfit like that," he said. "You ready for some pancakes?" He brought over some that were warming in the stove and moved the syrup and butter a little closer to my plate.

"Aren't you having any?" I said.

"I had some, I had some," he said. "I've been up for two hours now. Working around the yard. It's beautiful out."

126

I nodded, watching him. He really did seem different, happier. "What's up at the lot? Why are we going up there today?"

"Because it's some beautiful land up there, and we don't take advantage of it. Because it's a nice day. Because we should be reminded how lucky we are sometimes. How's that?"

I raised my eyebrows and took a bite of pancakes. "That'll do, I guess."

"We'll be back in time for the game," he said. The playoff game with Springfield was at four. "I figured we'd take the Model A."

"Sure," I said.

He shook his head, smiling. "There you go. Nothing exciting about a morning with dad, but the Model A'll get him out of the house." He put his coffee cup in the sink. "Finish your pancakes."

I poured some more syrup and ate. I told him I thought they were great, and he said he thought he'd surpassed himself this time.

"Whatever else your dad has trouble with," he said, "when it comes to pancakes it's strictly no contest."

"They never had a chance." I finished, put my dishes in the sink, and followed him out the door.

It was a beautiful day. Dad had the windshield open on the Model A — it pivoted upward so that you could open it if you weren't going too fast — and the wind was hitting us in the face. The hood gleamed and shone in the sun so that it hurt your eyes in spots, and we cruised through town, the morning air cool and the sun hot.

"Look at this day," he said. "Can you believe this? And you were going to sleep late. That would've been criminal."

I looked in the back. No saw, no rake for gravel. No idea as to what we were doing.

We passed through the other side of town and turned onto the interstate. We were going a different way this time, too. We chugged up the entrance ramp and stayed over in the right lane, cars flashing by us steadily. I always felt like a bit of a pain and a bit of a showoff in the Model A on the highway, like I was holding up traffic just so I could drive around in a weird car. A car behind us beeped and finally pulled out and passed us.

"Should we go a little faster?" I said.

Dad shook his head. "We're doin' all right."

I looked behind us. "It seems kinda slow."

"No, it's not slow. We're not driving a Ferrari here." He looked over at me and chuckled. "Don't expect this to be something it's not," he said. He looked back over the road. "This old buggy is what it is and that's all it can be."

We chugged along. After a while we turned off an exit ramp and headed away from the highway. The land went from farmland to forest, and from flat to a little more hilly, gradually, so that I was never really able to say just when the hills had started, once we were in them. We wound past houses that were noticeable only because their driveways connected with the road. Eventually we didn't see many homes at all.

"Most of this is state land," Dad said. "All behind our lot, away from the lake, is state land. I don't know what they're going to do with it."

"Maybe build a nuclear power plant," I said.

Dad rolled his eyes.

He stopped and turned off onto a little side road. We bumped along through the forest and up the hill, and finally pulled off the road at the edge of our lot.

The sun was coming down through the trees in beams you could follow. Birds were making noises in the clearing and I could see something small — a chipmunk — bobbing back and forth where a trail ran off into the woods. Some of the trees were just starting to turn, and oranges and yellows shone through here and there.

Dad got out and walked into the clearing, turning around, hands on hips. He smiled and shook his head and gestured toward the trees, as if there was really nothing more to say. I edged away from the car, happy he seemed so happy but really not sure what was going to happen next, in a way; it was so unlike him. He crouched in the middle of the clearing in the sun and let his hands dangle off his knees. I walked over and sat down next to him. You could hear the birds going from tree to tree.

"This is — " Dad shook his head. "This is just really nice."

I nodded, and looked back at the car, thinking about the empty backseat. "I still don't know what we're doing here."

Dad smiled. "You're a real nature lover, you know it?" He stood up. "All right, officer, it so happens I do have a reason for coming here. Your old man isn't turning simple yet. I got Freddy Baird coming out here to talk to me about taxes on the property."

"Taxes?"

"Taxes, taxes. We're gonna try and swing something. He's never seen the land; he's going to check it out. If I can get a break on something, maybe we can keep it."

"Really?" That's why he was in a good mood. "Is that all it would take?"

He shrugged. "Maybe. Think positive. Maybe not. If not, I'm going to give up the dealership."

My mouth dropped open. I leaned back on my elbows. "Give up the dealership?"

He laughed. "I didn't say I was going to give up life."

"What would you do? How would we make money?"

"How are we making money now? Nobody's

buying new cars. I sit around all day and talk to the secretaries. And lose weight over it." He scratched at some tree bark. "I'd open my own garage. We're not losing anything at the dealership on the service end of it, let me tell you."

"Won't that be hard, too?"

"Yeah. But cars'll always break down. Believe me. I'm selling 'em now, I know. And if we do a good job, we should do pretty good business. A lot of garages hand your car back to you in a basket."

He looked at me, waiting. "What do you think?"

I didn't know what to think. I didn't know what to think about first. "Great," I said.

"You know, I just assumed I'd have to get rid of this. And then last week I just thought — why? Would I get rid of the Model A? Why was I protecting the things that weren't important? And sacrificing the things that were?" He walked over to the Model A. "You got to change with the times," he said. "I raced. I fixed cars. That's what I really liked to do. When I look back on it, sometimes I don't even know how I got into this dealership."

He rapped the hood. "Anyway, that's it. End of speech. I've been talking it up too much." He turned. "Well, you can't say we don't talk anymore."

A car came up the road and stopped alongside the Model A.

"Freddie!" Dad said. "How's tricks?"

131

Mr. Baird got out and shook both our hands. We talked for a little while and then they headed for the overlook by the lake, and I said, "Dad, I'm going to check out this path, okay?"

"Don't wander off," he said.

I headed down the path at a pretty good pace, taking advantage of the downhill. Small branches and vines and things tickled my bare legs above the socks, and the sun and the smell of the forest made me feel like I wanted to check everything out at once. It started going uphill, pretty steeply, but I barely slowed down, scrabbling for balance at times, and when I crested the hill I looked around and it seemed like I was alone for miles in every direction. The sun was hot on my shoulders and my shirt was damp. I could smell the leaves in the heat. I trotted down the hill into some shade and came on a fork in the trail. One was much narrower, almost overgrown. I headed down that one. I walked after a while, worrying once that I might be away too long by the time I got back, but figuring I'd hear Dad yell anyway. I followed the slope of a long ridge a little ways and then the path left the ridge and I turned a kind of corner around some big oaks and stopped.

The sun was coming through the forest behind me and breaking up on the leaves and branches, and in front of me was a solid, huge stand of white birches, going for hundreds and hundreds of yards, it seemed, in all directions, every trunk I could see white and each one of them catching the sun and throwing it back at me, with their bright green leaves doing the same, and I backed up a step, afraid to go any farther because it was just so beautiful from where I was. Nothing moved. The white birches stood around me, and I walked into them. I walked until everywhere I turned there were clean white trunks, bright, beautiful, stretching up into the green leaves above. When the wind shook them, the sunlight shimmered. I was off the path, standing in some ferns. They were the ground cover, making everything I saw green and white. There was no brown or gray. All around me was pure green, with this thicket of beautiful white trunks, tall and thin and sweeping upward in criss-crossing lines.

I started to call Dad, but couldn't bring myself to raise my voice. I stood, not wanting to sit down, not wanting to move.

I heard a noise back toward the trail. I looked through the birches and something brown and huge moved past the white trunks, and out of sight.

I was staring off in that direction, listening with all the concentration I had, when it came right out of the birches next to me — a huge animal with a head that swept out toward me, and bones that stuck out high above its rear end: a moose. It stood next to me. I was looking into its eyes, set way back on the long head. I'd heard my father say once that moose looked like they'd been designed by a committee, and now I knew what he meant. Neither of us moved. It smelled like a wet dog. I thought, it looks funny without antlers, but that's all I thought. There was no noise. It snuffled toward me, and I had the feeling it was vaguely curious. I could hear one bird off in the distance. I could feel my tongue in my mouth.

The moose swung its head away, and went into the woods, and was gone. It was a big finish: a huge brown moose, in white trees, with a green background, gone with no trace. It moved faster than I thought possible, standing there watching it. It took me a minute to realize it was gone.

"I saw a moose," I whispered. "That was a moose."

I sat on a boulder that was magically there, hidden by the ferns. I just sat in the white birches. The breeze shifted the leaves and I felt like I was looking at everything through a clear stream. I thought about the moose and about Dad and the morning itself, and when I had picked out one particular birch and was following it up to the sky it came to me: I hadn't thought of Dean all day.

I leaned forward. I hadn't. And now, when I did, I wasn't surprised that I hadn't, and I didn't feel bad about him, either. I thought about Lisa and

Dad and what they'd been talking about, and I looked up into the sun, blinded for a second and grinning: I'd gotten it all wrong. We weren't growing apart; we were growing up. Both of us. And Dad, and Lisa — I'd never talked with them before. I never had to. If Dean hadn't made me, I never would have. I found out I didn't know Dean like I thought I did, but what else would have made me find out about Lisa or Dad? Or me?

I laughed to myself. And here I thought I'd be grateful to Dean just for making me improve my fielding.

I jumped up and tore down the path, leaping and slapping a birch trunk as I went by. A high five to a birch tree. I picked up the small path at top speed, branches whipping by, thwacking my arms or legs, and I turned onto the big path and came over the rise working up a good sweat but in no way going to slow down. I came crashing into the clearing and Dad and Freddie Baird were hanging around the cars, talking.

"I'm glad I told you not to wander off," Dad said. "Where'd you go, Ontario?"

"I saw a moose," I said. "And some birches. All these birches."

"A moose?" Freddie Baird said. "There haven't been moose around here for years. The only moose left are in the Upper Peninsula."

"It was a moose," I said.

135

"Sure it wasn't a horse?"

"It was a moose."

They looked at each other.

"It doesn't matter," I said. "There were all these birches — hundreds — and it was all white."

"Jeez," Dad said. "You don't just go into the woods when you go, do you?"

"It doesn't matter," I repeated. "Are you guys ready to go? Let's get back for the game."

"We're ready," Dad said, opening the door to the Model A. "I'll give you a call early Monday then?"

"Right," Mr. Baird said. "Hey, good luck today, Brad."

"Thanks," I said, barely hearing him as I slid in alongside Dad. "Let's get back," I said again, tapping the dashboard with my palm. "Let's get back home for the game."

Chapter 10
Dean

Springfield's Little League field was different than ours. They had parking on both sides of the diamond, and today the lots were jammed with cars, and there was a Good Humor truck behind the backstop. The whole thing was right next to the county dump; you could see it over the fence. Birds circled above it. I stood near the car, taking in the crowd, bigger even than the one at the Fremont game. There were people everywhere, walking back and forth, setting up chaise lounges and folding chairs next to the bleachers. Everything seemed strange, more hectic, exciting.

Most of the guys were already there. Mom wished me luck, and she and Dad went over to the bleachers and sat near Solly's parents. I went over and stood next to Herd.

"This is it," Herd said. "Hope you're ready to kick some tail."

I nodded.

Dwight came over and gave us both soul shakes.

"Just get me some runs," he said. "These dudes're through."

Kenny was stretching, spread out on the grass. John Hobbs was cleaning his glasses. Solly sat at the end of the bench, tapping one foot into the air. Coach was over past first base, talking with Randy Bell.

"Check this out," Herd said. He nodded toward the field. Springfield was taking batting practice. We watched what seemed to be the heart of their lineup. No one reached the fences. "Why are these guys supposed to be so good?" he said. "They don't even look as good as Fremont."

Coach came over to the bench. "Little lineup shakeup today," he said.

In the parking lot behind him was the red Camaro.

In front of the red Camaro was Dean, in his Adrian uniform, changing into his spikes.

"Here we go," Coach said. "Batting first, U.L. Second, Brad. Third, Kenny. Cleanup, Lawler. Dwight, fifth. Dean over there, sixth."

"Dean!" Dwight said. "We got Dean back?"

"Hey Brad," Herd said. "Check it out. Dean."

"I see him," I said. I looked over at the backstop. Randy Bell was cleaning off his spikes. It struck me that that was an awful thing to have to do — taking Randy out to put Dean in. Randy Bell had helped us get this far.

Coach looked over at me, and smiled. Had he known Dean had been coming back all along? "Seventh, Davey. Eighth, Solly. Ninth, Hobbs. We need a big pinch hit in the late innings, Mr. Bell is waiting," he said. "Right, Randy?"

"Yeah," Randy Bell said. He sounded grim.

Coach was all business but I could see he wasn't thrilled about having to sit Randy Bell at this stage, either. "Okay, now. Pay attention to the signs and pay attention to the situation." He sniffed at the air, and made a face. "Wind's blowing in from center, so anything hit straightaway'll be held up."

Dean was still over at the parking lot.

"How come he plays," Dwight said, "when he ran out on us before? 'Least Bell stuck around."

"Let's take care of this right now," Coach said. "I'm not taking a vote here. Randy and I talked it over" — Randy snorted — "and besides, it's not a team decision, or any one player's decision, it's the manager's decision. I want Bell on the bench where he can go in and get us a pinch hit or give us some defense if we need it, or even pitch for Robinson if he gets wild. Which you won't, right, Robinson?"

"The boy who's wild digs his own grave," recited Dwight, imitating Coach's voice. "Is there anything sadder than a base on balls?" Everyone laughed.

"The meeting's over," Coach said. "Gentlemen, I suggest you play ball."

The big kid from the Camaro stood next to Dean, talking and using his hands like he was gripping a bat.

"Who's that kid?" I asked.

"That's my brother," Davey said. "Who do you think?"

The big kid shook Dean's hand and walked over to the bleachers, and sat next to Mom and Dad. Dean came over to the bench.

"Hey, glad you could make it," Dwight said. "You gonna be around for the whole game?"

Dean nodded. "The whole thing." Some of the guys went over to clap him on the back and wish him luck. He looked over at me.

Coach was standing next to me. "He's been working out," he said. "Davey's brother's on Adrian High. Says he's been working with him every day."

"Why didn't he tell me?" I said, still looking at Dean.

"I don't know," Coach said. "When you get a chance, ask him. He only told me last night." He walked over to home plate to give the lineup card to the ump. He shook hands with Springfield's coach.

I went over to the bench and sat next to Solly. Everybody else was milling around, too keyed up to sit still. Solly's foot was tapping away a mile a minute. "Hey, Solly," I said. "Do you know Pearson's brother?"

"Yeah, I've seen him around. Why?"

"Where'd he get that brand new Camaro?"

Solly shrugged. "They're loaded. His dad owns a big farm out toward Ubly."

"That stupid Herd," I said. "He had me thinking the kid dealt drugs."

Solly looked at me. "Yeah. And I'm a hit man for the Mafia."

Randy sat on the bench, down at the end, by himself. I felt sorry for him. He was a nasty kid sometimes, but he always played hard and he liked to win. It was tough on him. He probably deserved to start. But I understood what Coach was doing: you've got to start your best team.

I looked over at the bleachers. Mom waved. Then Springfield took the field, running to their positions, and the people on both sides of us cheered. I shivered. Solly looked over, trying to smile and tapping his foot. Their pitcher was warming up and I could hear the popping of his pitches in the catcher's glove getting louder, sharper.

"Davey," I said, leaning down the bench. "You never told me your brother used to play for Adrian."

"You never asked," he said.

The ump said, "Play ball!" and U.L. grabbed a bat and headed out for home plate, all of us talking it up behind him. I grabbed my Louisville slugger and went out to the on-deck circle, dropping slowly to one knee. Behind me Kenny loosened up, swinging a few bats over his head.

U.L. stepped in, setting himself slowly and deliberately. Their pitcher was a tall, thin kid who looked like he had arms a size too long. He had a short, quick wind-up.

U.L. was bunting on the first pitch and the ball was on him before he was set, popping straight up in the air, twenty-five feet at least. He stared at it, starting to run down the first base line. The pitcher got it unassisted.

I patted him on the rear as he went by. I stepped in, fixed my grip, swung the bat back and forth. The kid wound up and fired. I swung and the catcher's glove cracked behind me like a board splitting. I looked over toward Coach. There was less talk coming from our bench. The kid fired again, and I just watched it. I had no time to swing. It was like the pitcher's mound was only half as far away. I dug in, thinking I'd have to commit myself sooner. He wound up and threw and the pitch dipped in the strike zone and I missed it by a foot.

I passed Kenny on the way back to the bench. "This looks serious," he said.

It was. That kid took Kenny down, *whap, whap,*

whap, on three pitches, three fastballs.

"Oh, Lord," Coach said. "First round of the playoffs, and we have to draw Sandy Koufax."

We took the field. Dwight gave up a hit right away and then the next guy up hit one deep to center, and Dean went back, back, back, and pulled it in. Beautiful. The guy after that grounded out to John Hobbs and the cleanup hitter popped back to Dwight.

We came back to the bench. "Okay, okay, way to shut 'em down," Coach said. "Now let's get some runs."

Herd went out there and took some serious cuts and then came back bouncing the bat along behind him, flopping down onto the bench. The kid had taken him out in four pitches. "That's how these guys are so good," he said.

Dwight fouled two off and went down swinging at a curve.

Coach put his hand over his eyes. "This kid's got four K's in five at-bats," he said.

I looked over to see Dean stepping in. He moved the bat back and forth slowly, setting himself and waiting. He took a curve for a strike.

"Let's go, Dean," Coach yelled. "Good luck," he said to himself.

Dean swung and missed another curve. I picked up my glove.

"Come on, Dean!" Dwight said. "Get something going!"

The kid put everything he had on a fastball, and Dean fouled it off.

Coach leaned forward. "Way to keep alive there," he said.

Dean stepped out, arranged his uniform, and stepped back in. The kid threw one high. Our bench was starting to talk it up again. Dean fouled another one off. The kid threw another ball.

"This might be the way to do it," Coach said. "We might have to walk our way on today." Dean fouled another one back. "At least he's making him throw a little," he added. The kid stepped off the rubber, took a breath, stepped back on, and cut loose with a wicked curve.

Dean got a piece of it, beating it into the ground, and they gunned him out. We cheered anyway.

"Awright, let's go," Coach said. "No runs."

They didn't get any. We took them down one-two-three, Kenny making a nice running catch near the left-field foul line for the final out.

Davey Pearson was looking at the end of his bat uncertainly, while Coach talked to him. "Make him work," he said. "Try and do what Dean did if you can't get something you can hit."

Davey struck out on three pitches. The last two were curves that looked like they were rolling off a table.

Coach gave Solly a grim look before he stepped

up to the plate. Solly got three fastballs and missed them all.

"Who is this kid?" Herd asked while John Hobbs headed out past the returning Solly. "Does anybody know?"

"What's it matter?" Dwight said. "Figure out how to hit him."

John Hobbs struck out.

"Another rally wiped out," Herd said, heading toward the plate with his mask.

Dwight struck out the first batter. He nodded toward the Springfield bench as if to say, You're not the only one around here who can do that.

The next kid drilled one over second for a base hit.

"C'mon, Dwight," Coach yelled from the bench. "Take your bows after the game. Pay attention to what you're doing."

Dwight made a big show of bearing down and got the next two guys to pop up.

"Awright," Coach said. "Top of the fourth. This is our inning. U.L., go out there and get on base."

U.L. struck out. Coach had a pained expression on his face.

I was next. I wasn't discouraged, which was weird. I was still thinking about the birches, and Lisa, and everything. I fouled off the kid's first pitch, which surprised and encouraged me. I got good wood on the second, and lined it into the third baseman's glove.

"I think we could get to this kid," I said back at the bench.

"Who knows?" Herd said. "Stranger things have happened."

Kenny made him work, too, fouling off pitches and protecting the strike zone, and drew a walk.

Our bench cheered him down to first. He was our first base runner.

"Rally, Herd," Coach said. "Here we go; rally starting."

Herd popped out.

We took the field. Dwight looked discouraged. "Don't worry about it," I said, passing the mound. "Really." I meant it.

Their first batter straightened out Dwight's third pitch, hitting a line drive right at me. I charged it, saw I wasn't going to reach it, and dropped to one knee, my glove down, concentrating on keeping the ball in front of me. I fielded it and threw it in to John Hobbs, holding the runner at first. Behind me Dean turned around and trotted back to his position.

Dwight struck somebody out, and then gave up a savage line drive that Dean charged without hesitating. I knew as soon as he did that he was going for the catch, not playing it safe, and I sprinted over to back him up. He dove, glove outstretched, and backhanded the ball. I watched him roll to his feet and throw it back in and I thought, Nobody plays center field like my brother does. I headed back to right. He glanced at me behind him and raised his eyebrows.

Hey, I thought. That's the way it is: You back me up, I back you up.

There was a crack and the ball came straight up toward me, a high, lofting fly, and I took one step forward and a few to my left and waited and made the put-out. No problem. I rolled the ball toward the mound on my way in.

Dwight grounded out to lead off our half of the fifth. He came back frustrated and dropped himself on the bench. I looked out at this kid.

He was taller than I thought, with a big, long face and short, black hair. He was sweating a lot but you could see that he was still working pretty easily, and looking at him, I wondered whether he'd throw a no-hitter at us. It was strange: I didn't dread it as much as just wonder it.

Dean was up again. The kid gave him a good look and then wound up and threw, and Dean lined it solidly between the shortstop and second base.

He held up at first and we were all up on the bench, cheering. I looked over at the bleachers and Mom and Dad and Davey Pearson's brother were up, too. Dean had our first hit. I thought about him, standing on first. All this time he had been working out, determined to get it right, determined to be more than half a player. That was Dean: He couldn't take not doing something right, absolutely right. I just never realized how much. He couldn't take not being the best he could be. And, it occurred to me, maybe back then I took it too well.

Davey Pearson stepped in and got a piece of a pitch but ended up striking out. Solly stepped in next and was fooled by the first pitch but got his bat on the second and looped it over the first baseman's outstretched glove. He flew across the bag, grinning from ear to ear, while Dean held up at second.

"That's my Solly!" his mother yelled from the bleachers. "Solly! Beautiful, Solly!"

Coach looked down the bench at Randy Bell. John Hobbs squinted back through his glasses from the on-deck circle. "What the heck," Coach said, "let's save it." He waved John Hobbs to go ahead.

John Hobbs dug in and took a ball, and then the kid threw three straight fastballs past him, and they were out of the inning.

"Well, so much for that idea," Coach said.

Dean and I crouched in center and right, watching Dwight mow them down in the bottom of the inning. He struck out the first two, and then the third batter hit one back to the fence in left that Kenny picked off the top like an apple off a tree. I trotted in from the outfield as proud of the Adrian Orioles and my part in them as I had ever been.

Coach seemed to feel it, too. "You guys are doing everything anyone could ask of you and more," he said. He looked out over the field, U.L. taking some practice swings with three bats. "You're the greatest."

"Once we beat this kid," Dwight said.

Coach shook his head, smiling. "No. Now."

U.L. stepped in against the kid, who looked tireder than ever. A drop of sweat hung on his nose and his green-and-white cap was soaked. U.L. looked cool, ready. The kid struck him out on three pitches.

I stepped in, dug a little spot for my right foot with my spikes. I can hit him, I thought. This kid's great, but I can hit him.

The kid stared at me, ignoring the sweat, his hair soaked, his chest soaked, and just kept firing them in. I missed one clean, fouled one off, and he missed outside with two. I stepped out; set myself again. He reared back and kept coming. I fouled off another two, and he missed high. It was a full count; he'd thrown seven pitches. He threw a sharp curve and I fouled it down the line. He threw another and took something off it and I struck out swinging.

I hesitated where my swing had left me, and then smiled, and sort of saluted him, touching my hand to my cap brim.

"What are you, the Red Baron out there?" Coach said when I got back to the bench, but he didn't sound mad. Kenny grounded out behind me.

When I walked back past Solly to right field he said, "Jeez, we could be here all day."

I whapped his arm with my glove. "I know," I said. I had this big smile on my face, and I wasn't even sure why. I trotted into right and set myself, and he was still looking over his shoulder at me.

Their leadoff batter hit a shot that ticked off Solly's glove and bounced toward me. I got my glove down and my knee behind it and it hit the heel of my glove and bounced up and off my leg. I was keeping them in front of me now. I threw it in to second and the runner held up at first. The next kid up hit a clean single to left. It occurred to me suddenly that they had a man in scoring position; they could score a run here. I leaned forward, concentrating. John Hobbs was creeping toward second, and suddenly he broke toward it: Coach had the pick off on, and Dwight spun around and fired low at the bag and they got him. Their coach was beside himself; he threw his clipboard in the air and turned away from the field.

The next kid up hit one down the line over first and I ran it down, playing it on the bounce almost in foul territory, and turned and planted myself. The kid was going for two. I threw hard and a little high for John Hobbs, who'd come out for the cutoff, and he pulled it down and fired to U.L., and we got him.

Dean looked over at me. "Hey," he called, grinning. "Where'd you learn to field?" There was a long moment while I appreciated what had just happened.

"Where'd you learn to hit?" I said. We both smiled, looking at each other. Dean took a few steps toward me.

"This kid always pulls it to right," he said.

"I know," I said. "He hasn't learned yet."

He straightened his cap and nodded. "Listen," he said, still watching the batter. "Everyone says I kind of messed up your head doing all this. I wanted to tell you I didn't want to do that."

"You did," I said. "And I still want to know why. Why did you do it? Why'd you quit?"

He shrugged. "Lot of reasons. *I* probably don't know them all. I guess I was tired of hearing 'Brad and Dean' like it was one name. That's one. And I hate it when I stink at something. I hate it when it doesn't go like it should. I hate it."

I thought about that. The kid at bat was fouling off pitches. "Well, I felt like that sometimes, too," I said. "But I didn't quit talking to you or going to games."

"I'm not saying I did the right thing," he said. "I'm trying to tell you why I did it. And I'm not sure" — you could see it was hard for him to say it — "I'm not sure we have to be best friends, forever."

I didn't say anything. He looked over, a little worried, I thought.

"That's all right," I finally said. It was hard to say. "But we don't have to be strangers, do we?"

He smiled and shook his head, relieved, and I was a little relieved myself. I flexed my glove and leaned forward. Hey. Just two pro baseball players here.

The kid fouled one off high and to the right, and out of nowhere came Herd, running flat out in front of the bleachers, trailing dust, and he shot out his arm on the dead run and pulled it in.

I trotted back in alongside Dean, elbow to elbow. We didn't say anything. For the first time in a long time, we didn't have to.

"This is it," Coach said. "Last inning. Jack one, Herd."

Herd did jack one, but he got under it a little, and they caught it in deep center, a pretty routine out.

Dean was sitting next to me on the bench. He got up and headed for the on-deck circle. "Let's go, Dwight," he called.

"Do it to 'em, Dwight," I said. Dwight managed to work the count to two and two before striking out.

"It's all right," Dean said. "We got time." He stepped into the batter's box, dug himself in, took a few swings to loosen up, and steadied his bat and waited. He pounced on the first pitch and drilled it. I thought it was gone. We all jumped up, screaming, but it hung there in the sky against the dump and the birds, just like Herd's did, and the center fielder had been playing Dean straightaway and deep. He took it in without having to move more than two or three steps.

We ran out for the bottom of the last inning somehow psyched by the near miss, not discouraged, realizing that this wasn't going to end, it was going to go into extra innings, and who knew how far into extra innings.

It was still as hot as it had been when we started. I looked up at the sky and I couldn't see any change from the way it had looked when we arrived. A perfect white cloud hung over the dump, just as I remembered it.

Dwight had a nice rhythm going and was just grooving them in. Kenny ran down a shot and pulled it out of the air. One out. Next. Dean caught one about knee high on the run with me cutting over behind him; made it look easy. Two outs. I looked across the outfield at them, amazed. Two outs, nobody on, and there was Dean, leaning forward, glove ready; and there was Kenny, standing relaxed and ready to run anything down;

and I thought, they're never going to score on us. This game is going to go on forever. I thought of Coach, saying we were the greatest already; I thought of the birches; I thought of Dad grinning in the clearing in the sun; I thought of Dean smiling at me and asking me where I'd learned to field. And I thought, If we never score, this game will never stop, and that's the most wonderful thing. It would be fantastic if we won, but it would be even better if those zeroes just kept coming, and we never stopped playing.

	1	2	3	4	5	6	7	8	9	R	H	E
Adrian	0	0	0	0	0	0	0	0	2	2	5	0
Springfield	0	0	0	0	0	0	0	0	1	1	9	0

Adrian:

	1	2	3	4	5	6	7	8	9	H/AB	R	RBI
Reed, ss	1			K		K			S	1/4	0	0
Harris, B, rf	K			5		K			S-R	1/4	1	0
Eades, lf	K			W		4-3			W-R	0/2	1	0
Lawler, c		K		2			8		6-2	0/4	0	0
Robinson, p		K			5-3		K		4	0/4	0	0
Harris, D, cf		5-3			S		8		S	2/4	0	2
Pearson, 3b			K		K			4-3	5-3	0/4	0	0
Ehrmann, 1b			K	S				4		1/3	0	0
Hobbs, 2b			K		K			3		0/3	0	0
										5/32	2	2

Springfield:

	1	2	3	4	5	6	7	8	9	H/AB	R	RBI
Lee, lf	S		5		S		5-3			2/4	0	0
Fried, 1b	8		6		S		1-3			1/4	0	0
Favale, c	4-3			S	S				D-R	3/4	1	0
Tanaka, 3b	1			K	2				K	0/4	0	0
Gordon, Jr, cf		4-3		8		7			S	1/4	0	1
Hawkes, 2b		6-3		9		8			8	0/4	0	0
Brody, rf		7			K	9			9	0/4	0	0
Rotondo, ss			K	K			8			0/3	0	0
Theobald, p			S	7				S		2/3	0	0
										9/34	1	1

About the Author

Scott Eller has always loved baseball and still plays whenever he gets the chance. He teaches creative writing at the college level. This is his first novel.